Dear Readers,

Mother Nature may have turned up the heat, but nothing could be hotter than four sizzling romances from Bouquet.

Get ready for two very different weddings! *Affaire de Coeur* raved about Suzanne Barrett's first Bouquet. This month she offers **Wild Irish Rogue,** a lively romp involving a green card, a favor of the matrimonial kind—and, of course, true love. In **The Bride's Best Man,** veteran Meteor author Laura Phillips gives us the story of a woman preparing to walk down the aisle—and wondering if her sexy childhood friend is really the man who should be at her side.

No one can pick out a bridal gown until she finds the right man—even if she finds him in the most unexpected place. A single dad is **Falling for Grace** in Maddie James's latest offering about neighbors who get close in the sweetest way possible. Finally, a legacy of love and a decades-old jewel heist provide the backdrop for one clashing couple's **Stolen Kisses** from Kate Donovan.

Why not pack a Bouquet in your beach bag and let us show you just how good romance can be?

Kate Duffy
Editorial Director

## FALLING FOR GRACE

Slowly, Carson moved back to Gracie's side of the bed. A quick remembrance of several nights earlier raced through his mind as he pulled the covers up around Gracie. No use in her getting cold in the night, he reasoned.

But he lingered there, as he'd done once before, so tempted to reach out and smooth baby-fine hairs away from her temples . . . as he'd done once before.

Her breathing was even and shallow, her lips slightly parted. Suddenly, Carson's thoughts were no longer on smoothing her hair away from her face, but on the softness of Gracie's lips and how they might feel, once again, pressed against his.

In the next instant, he found out . . .

# FALLING FOR GRACE

## MADDIE JAMES

Zebra Books
Kensington Publishing Corp.
http://www.zebrabooks.com

ZEBRA BOOKS are published by

Kensington Publishing Corp.
850 Third Avenue
New York, NY 10022

Zebra and the Z logo Reg. U.S. Pat. & TM Off.

First Printing: July, 2000
10 9 8 7 6 5 4 3 2 1

Printed in the United States of America

For my parents,
Evelyn and Russ Jacobs,
for a lifetime of supporting
my dreams.
I love you.

# ONE

*Tick. Tick. Tick.*

Gracie listened closely. She arched a brow and glanced toward the antique anniversary clock perched on top of the oak mantel she used as a display prop. Nope. It wasn't the clock, was it? She shook her head. It had to be. That damned, incessant ticking *was* coming from the clock. Right?

Wrong.

The clock didn't work and hadn't since she'd placed it there six years ago. She knew that as well as she knew her name was Grace Elizabeth Hart.

Damn but that blasted ticking wasn't in her own mind.

*Tick. Tick. Tick.*

Shaking her head she turned back to her work, only to end up staring at her computer screen, trying hard to dismiss the troublesome click. She tried to recall . . . when *had* it started? Last year? The year before that? She wasn't sure. But out of the blue one day that ticking just sort of erupted in the middle of her thoughts, and she knew right then and there what it was. No one had to tell her.

*Tick. Tick. Tick.*

Gracie slammed a hand down on the top of the old library table she used as a desk. "Oh, all right! What in the world do you expect me to do about it?" she said loudly. "I mean, it's not likely I can remedy the situation all by myself, can I?"

She stood and paced the room. No one answered her query, not even Claire, her calico shop cat, curled up into a lethargic lump in the storefront window.

No one had to tell her that the hands on her biological clock were swiftly sweeping the numbers.

Glancing about, she took in the shop around her. This was her second home. In fact, if she would go so far as to count up the hours, she probably spent more time here than she did in the apartment upstairs she called home. But that was to be expected.

After all, she was a businesswoman. And to run a successful business, one had to spend an enormous amount of time and effort in seeing that that business flew. Everyone knew that.

Especially during the first few years.

Well . . . ten years should more than do it, she guessed.

And with the time she put in to her shop, why in the world did she think she would have time for a baby?

*Tick. Tick. Tick.*

There could be no denying that Romantically Yours was a success. Everyone said so. Her accountant. Her best friend Amie. The members of the Chamber of Commerce. The Book Club. Why, even old Mrs. Talbot down the street complimented her every time she came into the shop to buy bath salts.

Yes, little Gracie Hart, homegrown and homespun, finally recovered from that awful experience in New York, was a success. Everyone in the small, central Kentucky town of Franklinville said so.

Then why didn't she feel like a success? And why was that incessant ticking still tapping away at her brain?

*Time. It's running out, Gracie.*

"Stop that. I know it. You don't have to remind me."

She turned her back on her computer and the anniversary clock then and stepped to the rear of the shop. Gracie poured herself a decadent rich cafe latte and sank into a '40s-style, overstuffed chair in the corner. She crossed her legs and perused her surroundings. Vintage clothing from the 1920s graced one wall. Reproduction Victorian jewelry dangled from a display rack on the counter. Aromatherapy products, from candles to bath salts to herbal sachets, were scattered about the shop.

On the back wall her collection of classic romance novels and other vintage books waited for adoring customers to lift them off the shelf and take them home. At the right back corner of the shop, one could order custom-designed gift baskets. Everything from chocolate to wine to lingerie could be included in the basket according to the taste of the receiver or the whim of the giver. Anything from her shop might do. Cards. Knick-knacks. Massage oil. Or any little trinket or one-of-a-kind antique accessory she had handpicked to be placed in her shop for the romantically inclined.

Reaching out, Gracie fingered an ivory crocheted doily sitting beneath a reproduction Tiffany lamp on a dark cherry table. She lifted her hand to carefully turn down the light. It was late—her shop had closed hours ago—and it was time to dull the day's events with some low lighting.

This was her favorite time of the day and her favorite corner for lounging and mulling. She had arranged an eclectic collection of overstuffed chairs and side tables where one could sit and peruse a novel, partake in tea and scones, or linger through her collection of catalogs from which she would special order. It was where the Book Club met on Friday evenings, the same five women, week in and week out. It was where her regular customers lounged and gossiped about the town's affairs.

Or if one preferred, which Gracie did quite often in the evenings, one could simply curl up in a chair and quietly reflect while a nice selection of classical music emanated from the CD player, incense wafted a light floral aroma, and candles flickered a soft glow about the room. A glass of wine added to that scenario was simply the créme de la créme. The only thing that came close to topping that was an hourlong bath in her clawfoot tub upstairs.

Romance surrounded her all day long. Her shop was her life, and it damned well had better be; it was the only romance she was getting. That was a hard pill to swallow for someone who was known as the local diva of romance.

*Tick. Tick. Tick.*

"Oh, shut up, won't you!"

"And to whom might you be talking?"

Jumping to her feet and grabbing her heart, Gracie whirled toward the voice. "Amie! You scared the heck out of me!"

Boldly stepping into the shop, Amie Clarke briskly rotated the key on the fake Tiffany lamp, turning up the light and harshly breaking the ambiance, then glanced around. "It's like a tomb in here, Gracie. Don't you want some light? And whom were you talking to? Yourself again? And shouldn't you be getting upstairs? It's way past ten. Oh, and you have to lock that back door; one of these days the boogey man is going to get you."

Sighing, Gracie stood, still trying to quiet her rapidly beating heart. She stepped toward her computer and muttered, "Perhaps I should let the boogey man in. He would be the first man to grace my back doorstep in quite some time."

"What? You were expecting a man to grace your doorstep?"

Gracie put the computer to sleep then eyed her friend and snorted. "Oh yeah, Amie. I was waiting for a clandestine liaison with the boogey man. He's hiding in the back room waiting for you to leave." She gestured toward the rear of the shop. "And do you ever *not* talk in circles?"

Amie smiled. "Never."

Gracie shook her head. "I know that already. You're like a bull in a china shop and a whirlwind all in one. You never shut up. You never make any sense." Gracie looked up at her friend then and smiled. "And you're about the best friend a girl could have."

Amie stepped up to the counter and fingered through some chocolate samples in a crystal candy dish. "Mind if I eat these? I'm starved."

Gracie shrugged. Again the subject was changed. "Help yourself. I'll put out fresh candy in the morning."

Amie smiled and munched for a few minutes and Gracie began closing up for the night. Going through the same motions she did every evening, she glanced about to make sure nothing was out of place and then stepped to the front door to recheck the lock.

Main Street, Franklinville was relatively quiet for this Thursday night, which was not uncommon. The street lights lent a warm glow to the late spring evening. A few vehicles passed by, but for the most part, the town was shut up tighter than a drum.

She glanced at the closed library across the street and up and down toward the other Victorian shop fronts lining the upscale, traditional little town sitting smack in the middle of Kentucky horse country. The cafes. The antique and craft stores. The fudge shop next door . . .

"So, when do you think you'll find a renter for the other side?" Amie called out, breaking the silence.

After a moment, Gracie turned and faced her friend, trying not to frown. She swallowed down the momentary upsurge of panic she always got when she thought about just that question. She didn't want Amie or anyone else to know just how crucial it was that she rent out the other half of her building. Financially, she relied on that rental income, and six months was too long for it to go empty without her pocketbook feeling the effects. "Hopefully tomorrow. Someone is coming to see the shop and the apartment in the morning."

Amie munched another caramel-nut candy and nodded. "Cool."


"Isabella, do you remember everything I've told you?"

"My name is Izzie."

Carson Price frowned. "Today it's Isabella. Now, do you remember?"

"Yes, Daddy. Of course I remember. You've told me a hundred times already. But do I *have* to wear this dress?"

"Yes, darling, you have to. Now buck up and be a good girl. Daddy is counting on this meeting today. Hear me?"

"But, Dad-dy . . ."

"Isabella!"

"Oh . . . all right," the child muttered.

Carson tried to ignore the rumbling under his daughter's breath as he eased off the exit from Interstate 64 onto U.S. Route 60 toward Franklinville. The trip from Louisville was only a little more than an hour but more than enough time for Izzie to get fidgety and start resenting the fact that she had to wear a dress today. And, he had to admit, he'd drilled the scenario for the morning's appointment in her head for way too long.

He wasn't quite sure where his head was earlier in the week when he'd made the appointment with Grace Hart. He'd forgotten that school was out today. He'd definitely not planned to drag Izzie along on this business venture, not today at any rate; but it seemed that she was destined to be here anyway.

Kate, his baby-sitter, was out of town and Carson was at a loss to find anyone else. It was his own fault, he knew. He'd totally forgotten to look at the school calendar and didn't realize the private school Izzie attended had scheduled a professional development day for the teachers.

Well, there was nothing to be done about it now. Izzie was here and he just had to hope for the best.

Mentally he crossed his fingers and sent up a silent prayer. Izzie was known not to do too well in social situations.

"Are we gonna move to this town?"

Carson glanced to his right and took in his daughter's questioning face. "It's possible, Iz. I don't know yet." They had talked about the prospect of moving, but not in detail.

"I don't wanna. I like my school."

Obviously. She ruled the roost there. Carson had to chuckle to himself. Izzie did have quite a following for a six-year-old tomboy.

"I'm sure you'll adjust, Iz."

"Maybe I could just stay with Kate."

Carson frowned. "Kate is your baby-sitter, honey, not your parent. You'll go where I go."

"But it's not fair!" The whining started.

"Of course it is. I feed you and clothe you and you and I are a team, remember, sport?" He reached over to chuck her arm and made a funny face, trying to get her to laugh.

Izzie sat silent for a moment and stared straight ahead. She didn't return the funny face or laugh with him. Carson let the subject drop and kept heading toward Franklinville.

"Can I at least wear my ball cap?" she said after a few minutes. "It keeps the hair out of my face."

"No!"

Carson glanced at his daughter and immediately wished he could retract that stern *no*. He reached out and touched the child's freckled face, then threaded his fingers through a thin tendril of curls. "Izzie, your hair is so beautiful, I want you to keep it down. Okay?"

She thought about that for a minute. "Is my hair like Mom's?" she finally asked.

Funny, Carson didn't prickle at those questions much anymore. "Honey, your hair is lighter, remember? But long like your mom's."

"Did you like her hair?"

"I loved her hair."

"Did you love my mom?"

Carson looked ahead and sighed. "Yes, Izzie, I loved your mom very much."

"Then why did she leave us?"

Why, of all days, this conversation? Carson thought

a moment, glanced at his watch, and then pulled over to the side of the road. He looked Izzie straight in the eyes and touched her cheek again and spoke softly. "Isabella, your mother didn't leave because I didn't love her enough or because you didn't love her enough. And she didn't leave because she didn't love you. In fact, she loved you so much that she had to leave, she felt, in order for you and me to be happy. She wasn't happy and she needed to go . . ."

"I know, I know," Izzie singsonged. "I've heard it before. My mom had to go off and find herself and become an actress and be happy. Well, is she happy, Daddy? How do we know? She never talks to us anymore."

Carson bit his lip and tried not to damn his ex-wife to hell and back. "I know that, honey. But you got a present from her at Christmas, right?"

Izzie huffed. "A stupid doll. Doesn't she know I don't like dolls? I wanted a football. And a card and present is not talking."

Carson closed his eyes and tilted his head back against the headrest. No, Marci wouldn't know that Izzie didn't like dolls because Marci didn't know her daughter. And Marci wouldn't understand that Izzie needed to talk to her mother because Marci was too obsessed with herself. But how could he tell his beautiful daughter that?

He couldn't.

Glancing at his watch again, he told her, "Honey, we need to get to Franklinville. Can we talk about this later?" He was avoiding the obvious and knew it, but he just didn't know how to respond.

Izzie turned toward the window and curled up into the corner. She was shutting him off. Oh God, he hated when she did that. There would be hell to pay later on. But there was nothing he could do about it now.

*Dammit, Marci! How could you do this to her?*

*Enough,* Carson told himself. Damning Marci and her acting career was not a priority at the moment. His daughter and her future—*their* future—was. Izzie was the reason he wanted to move to the small town of Franklinville and Izzie was the reason he was quitting his law practice—well, partially the reason, anyway. He was burned out beyond any hope of getting back the thrill of practicing law. He was gone way too much and Izzie was, to put it mildly, quite a handful at times. He'd been thinking for months about changing careers, changing lifestyles, and then his brother Joe had made a suggestion that he couldn't refuse.

His younger brother regularly traveled through Franklinville on his daily commute to work and had kept telling Carson about the shop for rent downtown. Joe had even stopped and looked in the windows one evening. He knew that since they were kids, Carson had wanted to own his own business, and kept telling him to think about it.

Carson knew he had enough of a nest egg put away to get started; money wasn't a problem. For years he'd thought he had to continue in the profession he'd worked so hard to attain and it was hard to let the legal profession go.

Then he realized he had to do it for Izzie. She needed him. And way too often, he wasn't there for her. Kate was more of a parent to her than he was.

Joe's suggestion kept nagging at him, day after day.

At the very least, he couldn't refuse looking into it.

Hence, the meeting today with Grace Hart. And it was imperative that Izzie cooperate, because he'd already made up his mind.

They were getting a new life in Franklinville, come hell or high water.

"Things are going to be all right, Izzie. I promise you," he said softly.

"Yeah, right," he heard her mutter back.


It was ten minutes after nine and Carson Price was late.

Gracie scowled as she glanced from her watch to the front door then back to her watch again. Punctuality was important to her. And she thought she'd made it perfectly clear to Mr. Price that they needed to meet at nine o'clock, or even before, so they could take care of business before her shop opened at ten.

And he had agreed. She was certain of it.

But it seemed he didn't think it was important.

One strike against Mr. Carson Price.

Turning, she stepped to the counter and counted the money in her cash register drawer, her foot tapping at the polished hardwood floor. "It doesn't matter, Gracie," she told herself. "What's a few minutes? Relax."

Taking a deep breath, she exhaled. Long.

"And besides, he could be money in the bank."

She really had to get out of this perfectionist mindset. It was going to drive her nuts.

Her head jerked up when the tapping sounded at her front door. "Thank goodness," she said under her breath. She could see a figure standing behind the mottled, stained glass window in the door and could only assume it was Carson Price. As she crossed the shop, she smoothed a hand over her skirt and straightened the sweater on her shoulders, then tipped her chin up and straightened her back to achieve her power posture.

Actually, it was her dancer's posture but she hadn't danced in years.

"Please let this work out," she whispered and sent up a small prayer.

Stopping briefly in front of the door, Gracie inhaled deeply then exhaled long, twisted the dead bolt, and opened the door fully.

She extended her hand without even really looking. "Mr. Price, I assume?"

Then she did look. Up. And up some more. My, he was a tall man. She gulped. He had to be tall for her to look up to him. She was nearly five feet, ten inches, herself. Her mouth and lips suddenly went incredibly dry.

Her eyes met the most unbelievable sea-blue eyes

she'd ever seen. Finally she felt something touch her palm.

"Oh!" She dragged her gaze away from his and glanced downward to her hand, now in his. His hand was warm, his handshake firm.

"Grace Hart?"

"Oh, yes." She looked back into his face. "Yes, I'm Grace Hart. Mr. Price?"

He nodded and she took in more of his features. Dark brown hair, chiseled high cheekbones, and those eyes . . .

"Yes," he answered.

"Please come in," she returned politely.

He stepped inside and she closed the door behind her, then felt it push open again against her rear.

"Forget something, Dad?"

Carson Price turned and so did Gracie. An imp of a child stood in the doorway, staring past her. Gracie guessed her to be about five or six years old. There was a frown on her face as she eyed her father, the doorway still framing her. Slowly, she crossed her arms over her chest and tilted her chin to look at Carson, a small look of defiance on her face. Her right foot repeatedly tapped the floor

Gracie was not quite sure what to make of the child. She glanced quickly to Carson, who returned a hesitant smile, then to the child.

The little girl's head held a mass of light brown curls which, if left loose, would most likely tumble halfway down her back, Gracie thought. Oh my, what she would have given, as a young girl, for curls like that. Oddly enough though, this child's locks were

caught up in a dusty, Louisville Cardinals baseball
cap, which contrasted sharply with the Sunday-best
frill she wore.

Gracie bent slightly to look the girl more closely
in the face. "Well," she finally said, pushing out her
hand, "I'm Grace. What's your name?"

"I'm Iz—"

Carson Price bolted forward. "Isabella," he returned, grasping the child's hand.

Gracie stood tall again and looked Carson in the
eyes. It was nice looking directly into a man's eyes
and not looking down at him for once. "What a
beautiful name."

"Thank you. Isabella is my daughter. There was
no school today. I hope you don't mind. My baby-
sitter was out of town."

Gracie shook her head. "Oh, my no. It's not a
problem."

She dismissed the issue of the child for a moment, then headed for the cash register. "Just give
me a second to grab the keys and I'll take you
next door."

An awkward silence filled the shop as Grace fumbled with the cash register drawer, her thoughts nowhere near where they should be.

Carson Price was not the kind of man she'd expected. No indeedy. He was much too—

No, she refused to think about it. After all, the
man had a child. Most likely there was a wife in the
picture somewhere.

Gracie sighed deeply.

With that thought, she retrieved the key from the

secret drawer inside the cash register. Gracie glanced up to see Carson crouched down on eye-level with the child, faint mutterings of conversation going on between father and daughter.

"Ready?" She stepped up behind them and Carson rose quickly to his feet, snatching the ball cap off his Isabella's head on his ascent. Gracie registered a sharp glance of annoyance from the child and the stern, warning stare back from the parent as he quickly stuffed the ball cap into the back pocket of his khaki pants. "We'll take a look at the shop first, then the apartment," she continued.

"That's fine," Carson Price replied.

"Unless, of course, you'd rather wait until your wife could come to look at the apartment."

He shook his head. "No wife, just us."

Gracie nodded. "Oh. Well, right this way then." She extended a hand toward the front door.

Carson Price led the way, daughter in tow, and Gracie found herself watching those nicely fitting khakis from the rear until he opened the door and held it for her to pass through.

No wife. This wasn't a good sign.

No indeedy.

There was a brief tingle as she brushed past him and Gracie wondered from just where that tingle sprang up. She'd not felt anything like that in—oh, in quite some time. Years, if she cared to admit it.

And she didn't want to admit it.

She decided right then and there that renting to Carson Price was probably a bad idea. He was much too handsome and much too charismatic. He had an adorable little child. And no wife.

Two strikes against Mr. Carson Price.

No. Strikes two, three, and four.

# TWO

This was a bad idea. A very bad idea.

Carson lifted one eyebrow and glared another warning at his daughter. Her tilted chin and shining eyes flared a defiant challenge right back.

*Be good*, he mouthed behind Grace Hart's back.

Izzie grinned sweetly—a grin he knew meant anything but sweetness—and followed along beside her father, desperately trying to keep in his stride.

Big, tough, little girl, he thought. What in the world made her that way? Was it him? Marci's leaving? What?

He tried not to think about it. Surely Izzie wouldn't turn on her shenanigans this morning. Of course, if that ball cap trick was a precursor of things to come, he wanted to be prepared. Sometimes Izzie turned on without warning. Other times she worked herself up to it. And her moody behavior in the car earlier was probably the first subtle warning that things might go terribly, terribly wrong today.

Oh hell. Not today. He was counting on today working out.

Pull it together, Price, he told himself. Trust that Izzie will be okay. Concentrate on the thing at hand.

And remember. This is *for* Izzie, even if she doesn't know it or understand it.

Yet.

He forced himself to focus on the tall, willowy female in front of him. Perhaps force wasn't the right word. Grace Hart was very easy on the eyes and nothing like he'd pictured. Of course, he'd only spoken to her on the phone, and briefly at that, a few days earlier. Her voice was pleasant and young-sounding and he'd be a liar if he hadn't conjured up thoughts about what the face behind that voice might look like.

But he hadn't pondered it for long. He'd been way too busy the past few days trying to tie up loose ends. His small, private law practice was consuming all his time, as usual, even though he'd already started handing over projects to his associate Jack Roberson. The other half of Roberson and Price.

He wanted out. Jack knew it and was more than eager to take up the slack Carson had tossed his way the past few weeks. Even though he had not a clue what the coming months would offer, Carson did know that he had to get out of Louisville and he had to get out of practicing law. And soon. His biggest fear was that Izzie was making a beeline directly to six-year-old self-destruction. He was hell-bent on turning the child around.

A new town. A new career. A new way of life. That's what he wanted.

He blamed himself; he refused to blame Marci any

longer. The lengthy hours at the office, the hours later at home where he practically ignored his daughter—those were the things he blamed. Not Marci's leaving. His pattern of the past three years had to change and change dramatically. Izzie was his priority now and he'd be damned if anything or anyone would stand between him and his daughter's well-being.

"Well, this is it."

Grace turned and smiled as she pulled the key from the lock and swung the door into the shop. Carson gave himself a mental shake, pulling his thoughts back to the task at hand. But at that point he felt something else, something foreign pull and tug in his chest. Subconsciously sweeping it away, Carson motioned for her to step inside. Watching her let herself into the shop in front of him, he allowed a brief sigh to exit his lips.

She was a graceful beauty whose name suited her well.

"It really has a nice layout," Grace said as she led him further into the room. He watched the slight sway of her hips as she moved ahead of him. Her movement reminded him somewhat of a feather being blown forward.

"The front room is large enough for just about any kind of shop or cafe or what-have-you. There is a nice storage area in the rear, which I'll show you in a minute, and a small bathroom. And of course, as I mentioned, the apartment upstairs goes with it."

She stopped and he sensed her staring at him.

"Mr. Carson?"

He glanced away and cleared his throat. No, he'd been wrong. It was he who was staring at her.

"Yes, it is a nice layout."

He glanced about the room, taking mental notes as he panned the area. Yes, it might just do. It needed some work, but he wasn't afraid of hard work. In fact, after sitting behind a desk the past several years, he was looking forward to some mindless labor. He could almost feel the weight of a hammer in his hand.

"What about water? Other than the bathroom, I mean. Any problem with piping some plumbing into this main room?"

Grace Hart tossed a baffled glance his way, then looked out over the room again. "Water? In this part?"

"Just for a . . . a serving area." He glanced to his right, to the wall dividing his shop from Grace's. "Maybe over there, against the wall."

She followed his gaze. "Serving area? So, you are thinking of a restaurant or a cafe, Mr. Price?"

Carson swallowed. "Cafe. Yes." Well, it wasn't exactly a lie, he told himself.

Suddenly, her face brightened. "That's perfect! The little soup-and-sandwich place down the street closed a few months ago; so if you open up down here, it's sure to bring more business this way! I'm sure the Chamber of Commerce will be thrilled."

She smiled broadly in acceptance of his so-called plan. Carson felt a twinge of guilt, then pulled his gaze away from Grace Hart's face. Panning the room, he tried to take his mind off his pseudo-lie and picture the plan that was in his mind, mentally transferring it to the space before him.

Yes. It will do.

He wanted it badly. Badly enough to let a little white lie slip between his lips to get it.

"It's nearly perfect," he said quietly, more to himself than to Grace Hart.

"It's ugly, Dad."

Horrified, Carson looked sharply at Izzie. "Young ladies are to be seen and not heard." He bit out the warning, mentally chastising himself for being so blunt.

A small pained expression etched over Izzie's face, tearing at his heart. Immediately, he reached out to touch her face and started to apologize. She jerked away.

"Well, you know, I'd really have to agree, Isabella."

Grace laughed feebly; Carson slowly turned his gaze back to her. His heart, however, was heavy with Izzie's pain. Damn him. He'd gone and done it again.

"The last tenants left quickly and didn't do a very good job of cleaning up. I've just been putting it off. Of course I'll have it cleaned before you would rent."

"Still doesn't give a child the reason to voice her opinion," Carson offered.

This time Grace's face held the puzzled look. "Really, it's all right. She was just saying what she thought. There is no harm done."

Carson glanced back at his daughter. "I'd like for you to apologize to Ms. Hart, Isabella."

"Really, there is no need."

Carson ignored Grace and held his daughter's gaze. "Isabella?"

Izzie peered up at him through curled bangs. She held his stare for a minute, then slowly turned to look at Grace. "Sorry," she muttered.

Carson didn't think she meant it.

An instant later, Grace Hart stepped closer to Izzie and crouched down so that she was eye-level with the child. Carson watched as Grace took one of Izzie's small hands in her long, slim fingers and smiled.

"Apology accepted," she said, patting Izzie's palm. After a moment, she continued, "But I perfectly understand what you mean, Isabella."

"Izzie," the child corrected.

Grace nodded. "Oh yes, of course. Izzie. It's a wonderful name, you know? I really like it."

Carson watched as a smug, little expression sprouted across his daughter's face. "So do I," she returned.

Grace smiled broadly and Carson felt something catch in his chest. Her smile was one to be liked. Pleasant. Warm. Soothing almost.

Izzie must like it, too, he thought, because she was grinning right back at her.

"You know," Grace began again, searching Izzie's face, "I bet a girl like you would like a little snack about now." She glanced at the watch on her delicate wrist. "In fact, it's almost ten o'clock. I think a midmorning snack is in order. What do you think?"

Izzie cocked her head to one side and squinted. "Well, I did have an early breakfast."

"Well, that clinches it!" Grace dropped Izzie's hands and stood. "Over in my shop, back in the corner where the big chairs are, there is a plate of cookies and a pot of tea. You do like tea, don't you?"

Izzie frowned. "Hot or cold tea?"

"Well, it's probably lukewarm by now but I'm sure it's just fine for you. It's chocolate-raspberry." Grace smiled again. "I'm sure you'll like it."

She glanced to Carson then and motioned toward the door. "Please help yourself, Izzie."

Carson watched his daughter's gaze dart from him to the door, saw her tongue rake over her lower lip and her eyes glaze over in the hopes of a sugar rush. He had to head this one off at the pass.

He reached out and snagged Izzie's arm before she got away. "That's very kind of you, Ms. Hart, but—"

"Please don't tell me you're one of those parents who deprives your children of sugar, Mr. Price." Her eyebrows arched in anticipation of the answer.

Carson swallowed the words on his tongue. "Well, actually—"

"That's what I thought." Grace crouched down to look Izzie in the eyes again. "Now why don't you run along and find those cookies and the tea so your father and I can talk business for a few minutes. We'll join you in a little while."

Izzie's eyes met Carson's once more. Briefly.

"Okay!" she replied and then was off in a flash.

"Izzie!" Carson started after her.

"She'll be fine, Mr. Price."

"But you don't understand." He started toward the door.

"Mr. Price."

Carson felt a warm hand on his lower arm and it threw him momentarily off-kilter. He glanced down and took in the slim fingers resting there.

"She'll be fine. I promise. Now why don't you and I finish looking over the shop and get down to business."

Carson Price met Grace Hart's eyes again for about the hundredth time in the past fifteen minutes. This time, however, their gazes seemed to interlock and mingle and play some sort of betcha-I-can-hold-the-stare-longer game.

Suddenly, Carson was only thinking of one thing. Just what kind of business did Ms. Grace Hart really want to get down to?

He was misreading her, he was sure.

Grace Hart was all business, right down to the core. Feminine? Yes. Savvy? Definitely. Sophisticated? Absolutely. Sexy? Well, yeah. That, too. But he was trying not to think about it.

Above all, she'd showed some heart and compassion with Izzie a few minutes earlier.

There was definitely more to Ms. Grace Hart than business, but business was the name of the game at the moment. Nothing less, nothing more.

Izzie. My God. The havoc she could wreak next door. Praying that she would behave, he turned away once more to glance toward the door still open to the street.

It was at that instant he heard the tinkering, lingering, oh-God-don't-let-that-be-what-I-think-it-is crash—then an impish shriek followed by a loud, childlike gasp.

He knew that shriek and gasp all too well.

Abruptly, he turned back to Grace Hart's face and watched her eyes grow rounder than the elegant saucers he'd spied on the dainty table with the fancy cookies and the delicate teapot in the prim and fancy shop next door a few minutes earlier.

Oh, hell.


"Izzie!"

Gracie watched as Carson Price took off in a flash toward her store. Her heart had leapt to her throat just seconds earlier at the thought of poor Izzie lying in the midst of shards of glass and splinters of china.

She raced after Carson.

It was her fault. All her fault.

*Dammit!*

He'd tried to stop her, tried to tell her he didn't want his child to have cookies and tea. But no-o-o-o-o. She'd had to push the issue. Some minute, maternal instinct had wormed its way to the surface and manipulated her into plying the child with cookies and tea, which now, of course, was leading to disaster.

Her brain was spinning like a Tilt-a-Whirl.

Oh, Lord, she silently prayed, please let the child

be all right. And please let Carson Price not be too mad. And please let this be just a minor little skirmish that won't prevent him from wanting to rent the place from me.

She didn't really understand why, but she needed Carson Price. She needed him to rent the place next door and she needed him for—oh hell, some reason she really didn't quite understand yet. But more than that, she had the distinct feeling that he needed her. Izzie, too.

When and where she'd decided that, she wasn't quite sure. Perhaps it had something to do with the way Izzie had looked into her eyes a few minutes ago.

Gracie rushed through the door and into her shop. Damn, damn, damned maternal instincts! she chided herself.

*What the hell do I know about maternal instincts? For all I know, mine could be cracked off-kilter, since the opportunity to be maternal has not yet once presented itself into my life.*

She entered her shop just behind Carson and raced to the back. Her eyes darted back and forth, scanning the room, trying to find Izzie. She didn't see her.

Carson stopped abruptly in front of her and she plowed into him from behind with an *oof!*

"Sorry," she said as she planted her feet and peered around him. Carson, unmoving, didn't answer.

She glanced at the table. The glass inset piece teetered off the edge.

The place was a mess.

Her teapot was a goner.

The cookies were smashed to smithereens.

Her favorite cookie plate was now in three distinct pieces.

And even worse, it seemed upon closer inspection, that Izzie had vamoosed.

"Izzie!" Carson bellowed out sharply.

Gracie backed up, the sound of his stern voice startling her. She studied him from the side. Etched into his face was worry and anger and frustration—and a host of other things, probably, that she couldn't quite define. The tendons of his neck were taut and prominent and his jaw was firmly set.

"Isabella!"

Silence. Gracie slipped her gaze away from Carson's face to pan the room again, more slowly this time. Izzie couldn't have gone far; there wouldn't have been time.

Unless, of course, she'd slipped out the back door.

"Isabella Price!"

Carson was still unmoving, as though he'd played this game before with his daughter and that the rules of the game were, when he bellowed, she jumped. Well, so far, Izzie wasn't jumping.

She wondered when the middle name—

"Isabella Marcia Price!"

There. There it was. Gracie now wondered if the child would appear.

More silence.

Slipping away from Carson, Gracie edged toward the back of the shop. He bellowed out his daughter's name once more and she had to wonder why he thought the girl would come out of hiding with sub-sequent bellowings if she hadn't emerged after the first one.

Perhaps paternal instincts were somewhat differ-ent from maternal ones.

Mentally shrugging, Gracie traveled quietly to-ward the rear of the store, silently easing her way through the half-open door, and glanced to her right into the storage room.

Her shop was the mirror image of the one next door. Carson's had the storage area to the left, bath-room to the right. Hers was the opposite. They shared the back stairway that led to the apartments above each shop. The bathrooms were actually tucked beneath that stairway.

Funny, she was already thinking of the shop and apartment as Carson's. Hmmmm . . . She shook off that notion and got back to the task at hand.

Upon quick inspection of the storage area, Gracie realized that Izzie wasn't there. She supposed she could have hidden behind some boxes or under-neath her worktable, but she didn't think so. She sensed, more than actually observed, that the child was not there.

Gracie turned to her left.

The stairwell was empty but something drew her to it. At that point Carson came bursting through the door beside her. He was about to bellow out again, but Gracie put a finger to her lip and tossed him the most urgent look she could muster. He stopped dead in his tracks, a bit perplexed it seemed, and waited.

It was then that she noticed the smear of blood on his forefinger. It looked as if he'd wiped it off the floor or the table; it was laced with crumbs and sugar.

"Wait here," she said to him, pleading more with her eyes than with her words. Suddenly, she was frightened for Izzie. Considering the bellowing that man had done earlier, she didn't want him to frighten the girl any further.

Silently, she crept up the stairs, carefully avoiding the steps that creaked, a trick she'd learned over time. Her last tenant of six years had complained incessantly about her climbing the stairs to her apartment late at night after she'd finished her workday, waking him every time.

She made the first landing, then followed the stairway's angle to the left. There she found the child hunched near the wall, clutching one hand with the other, a small trickle of blood oozing out between her fingers.

"Izzie, you're hurt." Gracie crouched down in front of her. "Let me see."

The child looked lost and confused at first, not to mention a bit vulnerable; then her eyes caught sight of her father moving up the stairs behind Gracie.

Izzie puffed up her chest, set her jaw, tilted her head, and stuck both hands behind her back.

"Ain't nothin'," she remarked.

Gone was the frightened little girl of a second ago. In her place was one tough little lady.

Glancing over her shoulder, Gracie sensed the reason for that tough exterior. If he bellowed one more time, she told herself, she was going to bellow right back at him.

But he didn't. Crouching down beside her, getting closer to his daughter, he reached out his hand. "Izzie, let me see, honey."

Gracie looked at Mr. Carson Price again. His face was ashen and beads of perspiration were popping out on his forehead. He was worried. And scared. He may just have redeemed himself in her eyes, Gracie thought.

"Okay, baby? Let me see what you did," he crooned softly to the child.

"Ain't nothin', Dad. It will be okay."

"You're bleeding."

The child shrugged. "No big deal."

"Yes, it's a big deal. You're hurt and I want to help you. Let's take a look at it."

Isabella Marcia Price glanced from her father to Gracie and then back to her father again. After a moment, she slowly pushed her hand forward.

The fleshy part of her palm, right below her thumb, sported a small cut. Gracie noticed that the child's eyes never left her father's.

Gingerly, he took her impish hand in his large one and cradled it there.

"This has gotta hurt a bit, Iz. I know it has to."

She nodded slightly.

Gracie leaned forward. She thought she saw something glimmer in the child's hand, a reflection of the overhead stairwell light.

"I think there is a piece of glass in there," she offered.

Carson looked at Gracie and then back to study his daughter's palm. "I think you're right. Do you have a pair of tweezers around here anywhere?"

Nodding, she replied, "Sure do. Let's head upstairs to my apartment."

Gracie realized then, just as those words escaped her mouth, that this was the first time she'd invited a man into her apartment in, oh, about a thousand years. She wasn't quite sure she was prepared for it, but there was definitely not time to mull over that situation at the moment.

There were more pressing things at hand.

# THREE

"You don't have to carry me, Dad. My legs ain't hurt."

"Aren't hurt."

"The glass is in my hand, not my leg. Put me down now."

"I'll put you down in a minute. I don't want to risk your tripping and breaking your fall with that hand."

"But—"

Carson stopped at the stop of the stairs, narrowed his gaze, and looked into his daughter's face. "But what, Iz?" he replied with a huff.

Izzie smirked. "Nothing, Dad."

Carson wasn't quite sure what made him so scared—the fact that Izzie had momentarily disappeared, that the sight of her blood drops on the floor had rendered him nearly incapable of functioning, or the thought that Grace Hart would now never rent to him.

Truth be known, it was a mixture of all three, with extreme emphasis on the blood issue. His heart leapt into his throat every time he thought about Izzie bleeding and him not being able to find her.

He held her close and waited while Grace opened the door to her apartment, then showed them into the kitchen.

"The light in here is better," she said. "Why don't you set her there on the counter and I'll go get tweezers and some peroxide?"

Carson nodded and followed her instructions.

The small kitchen was bright and airy, cheerful and welcoming. In fact, the whole apartment appeared to be that way. It smelled nice, too—like lemons and cinnamon. He didn't know about the combination, but he liked it. He'd noticed all that as soon as he'd stepped over the threshold—even though his primary thoughts were still on Izzie's wound.

"Let me see that, Bubblebuns." He cradled Izzie's small hand in his, then looked into her eyes.

"Don't call me that."

Carson frowned at his daughter—whose face still held an unhappy expression—then tossed a teasing wink at her. Finally, after a moment of scrutinizing him, she winked back.

"I'll call you anything I darned well please," he added with a hint of a grin. "You're my Bubblebuns."

Izzie laughed, her smirk fading fully into a broad smile.

"Dad," she began. "It was an accident. The cookies, I mean."

"Later," he told her, then turned his concentra-

tion on her wound. He'd settle up with Grace about
the damages later. And he'd settle up with his
daughter about the damages much later, with a long
talk and some extra chores to earn enough funds
to pay him back for replacing the delicate china
she'd shattered.

He just hoped it wasn't priceless.

Grace reappeared with a damp washcloth, ban-
dages, cotton balls, tweezers, and hydrogen peroxide. "Here, I think this is all we need."

She set the items on the counter—fumbled the
peroxide, then righted it again quickly—then simultaneously looked up into Carson's eyes and bit her
lower lip.

"Thank you," he replied.

She was nervous. For the life of him he couldn't
figure out why, but she was. Her hands were shaking
as she laid the items on the counter. Funny, a self-
assured businesswoman like herself didn't seem the
type to be nervous about much, he thought. But for
some reason, there was a slight change in her demeanor. Not quite able to put his finger on it, he
glanced back to Izzie and stared once more at the
child's palm.

"Would you like to do the honors, or shall I?"
Grace offered.

Carson realized then that he'd made no move to
pick the glass out of Izzie's hand and that, while he
was studying his child's wound, he was also wondering what the woman standing beside him was all
about.

*Mind to task, Carson.*

"I'll do it," he returned. Never let it be said that Carson Price didn't take care of his own.

"Do what?" Izzie queried.

His eyes met his daughter's once more. "There is a little piece of glass in there, Iz. It has to come out. It won't hurt, I promise. And then we'll clean it up and bandage it and we can get on with our day, okay?" He reached for a cotton ball and the peroxide. "And if you're real still and quiet and good, I'll even treat you to lunch."

Turning to Grace, he said, "I'm sure there's a McDonald's around here somewhere, right, Ms. Hart?"

Grace looked at him—a rather odd little look, as if he'd grown another head or his ears had suddenly sprouted points or something. She didn't answer.

"Ms. Hart?"

"Gracie," she answered.

*Gracie.* The word flowed off her lips and landed feather light on his brain. Gracie. He liked the sound of that.

Suddenly she shook her head, as if she were shaking herself out of a trance, and said, "Grace, I mean."

Puzzled now, Carson stood a little straighter and peered into the eyes of the woman who stood before him. "So which is it? Grace or Gracie?" She looked puzzled herself, which was almost as amusing at it was endearing.

Carson felt at a loss for words, a little light-headed, and, surprisingly, a whole lot like smiling. Smiling like a fool. It was as if something had clicked deep down inside him and had pleasantly turned this disaster of a morning into something—

Something he didn't want to think about.

He looked at Iz. *Task at hand, Price.*

"My name is really Grace, but everyone calls me Gracie. I mean . . . my friends call me Gracie."

Slowly, he turned back to look at her. "Oh" was all he said. What else could he say? May I call you *Gracie,* too? Will we be friends? Even though my daughter just smashed your china teapot, crushed cookies into your polished hardwood floors, and obliterated one very expensive-looking cookie plate? Can I call you *Gracie?* Huh?

For some reason, he did want to call her that. Yes. For some crazy, insane notion, he wanted to get to know Ms. Grace Hart well enough to call her *Gracie.*

*Idiot!*

Gracie wasn't quite sure what was happening. Maybe she was getting sick. The flu *had* been going around. Her hands were shaking and her heart was pounding and she felt just a little bit light-headed. Thank goodness Carson Price had stopped looking at her and was now concentrating on getting that minute piece of glass out of his daughter's hand.

Get a grip, she told herself.

This was all very unnerving.

She knew what it was, although she hated to admit it. It wasn't the flu or a bad fish sandwich or anything of that nature. What she was feeling right now could only be attributed to one thing: There was a man in her kitchen.

A real live, muscular, drop-dead-gorgeous, intelligent man with eyes like she'd never in her life seen.

And his occupancy in her small galley kitchen seemed to suck the very air out of the room.

He made a commanding presence. A bit overwhelming and more than a little overpowering. Larger than life. When she'd returned with the first aid supplies, caught unaware by the sight of him, her entire body had gone into stupid mode.

She wracked her brain trying to recall the last man who had stood in exactly that spot. Right there. Occupying that narrow space between her counter and the refrigerator.

Pathetic, she told herself. Gracie Hart, you are pathetic.

Truth be known, she was worse than pathetic. She was thirty-five years old and couldn't remember the last time she'd entertained a man in her apartment.

Years. Ages. Aeons.

Pathetic.

She might as well just dry up and blow away.

"Ow!"

"Got it!"

"You did?" Gracie stepped forward just as Carson lifted the tweezers into the air. She studied the small piece of glass held between the tweezer points in his hand.

"I'm bleeding, Dad."

Glancing back to Izzie's hand, Grace caught sight of the thick bubble of blood oozing up out of the wound. She grabbed the damp washcloth and covered the cut, applied some pressure, and cradled Izzie's small hand with her own.

Somehow, Carson's hands simultaneously ended up around hers.

Surprisingly, she felt *his* hands shaking.

He jerked them away again quickly and said, "Oh! You have that? Okay . . . I'll fix a bandage." He then proceeded to busy himself with cutting a swatch of sterile gauze. He dropped the roll of gauze once, then twice. Gracie tried to concentrate on Izzie rather than on the fact that her father seemed to be having a heck of a time managing the bandage.

"You like cheeseburgers, Ms. Hart?"

She looked at Izzie. "What?"

"Cheeseburgers? You like 'em?"

Studying the child's impish face, Gracie's heart suddenly turned warm and fuzzy. Isabella Price was a beautiful child with an animated face and big ol' Disney-character eyes. She was looking at her now, those huge blue eyes full of question.

"Well, do you?"

Gracie hadn't eaten a cheeseburger since she was sixteen. "I love them," she replied.

"Me, too. Wanna come with us to McDonald's?"

Gracie felt her own eyes widen at the question. "Me?"

"Yeah."

Her heart suddenly didn't feel warm and fuzzy anymore, but lurched abruptly into panic mode. She glanced at Carson, who had finally managed to cut the bandage and was looking at her with an unreadable expression on his face, then back to Izzie. Sharing kitchen space was bad enough at the moment; she wasn't up for a cozy lunch for three at the neighborhood kid hangout.

"I . . . well, thank you, but perhaps another time."

"I'm sure Gracie has to stay with her shop, Iz."

*My shop? Yes. I have to stay with the shop. Did he call me* Gracie?

Nodding profusely, she agreed. "Yes. That's right. I need to stay with my shop." The shop which, she suddenly realized, was standing wide open to the street with no one manning the cash register. "And I really should be getting back down there."

Slowly, she removed the washcloth and pushed the child's hand toward Carson. "Perhaps you should take over from here."

"All right," he replied. He glanced to his daughter. "Don't you have something to say to Ms. Hart before she leaves, Iz?"

Izzie screwed up her face and slowly turned to look at Gracie. "Sorry," she finally whispered.

"I know," Gracie returned, then smiled back. "It's okay. I'm just glad you weren't badly hurt." She turned quickly back to Carson. "I . . . um . . . really do need to get back down there. The shop is open."

"I understand."

She retreated two more steps. "Help yourself to whatever you need."

"We'll be fine and will join you in a few minutes."

"Oh, sure." She was nearly in her living room now. "And we'll finish our business then."

"Yes."

"Good."

"Okay."

Then Gracie left. She tripped over the throw rug at the entrance to her door and nearly turned her ankle on the first step down the stairway. What in the world was wrong with her? Obviously, stupid mode had traveled down to her feet.

Stopping at the first landing, she paused, allowing a couple of thoughts to collect themselves in her head.

At that point she decided that she hoped stupid mode wasn't going to bounce back up to her heart. She'd kept such tight control over that heart for such a long time, it would be a shame for it to do something stupid, like get broken over a guy like Carson Price.

"Your change comes to two dollars and sixteen cents," Gracie told the young woman on the other side of the counter. The woman took her change, the aromatherapy candle she'd just purchased, smiled, then leisurely left the shop.

Gracie watched her leave then made a mental note to order more of those candles. This was something new from a different supplier and that particular brand was flying out of the shop faster than she could keep them in stock.

Turning, she glanced about and decided that instead of a mental note, she needed to make reference to the candles in her computer inventory software program before she forgot about it.

She booted up the computer and glanced once more at the back stairway. Twenty minutes earlier she'd left Carson and Izzie upstairs. She'd seen neither hide nor hair of them since.

Odd, she thought, hoping that Izzie was okay.

"He's probably still fumbling with the bandage," Gracie said to herself, then chuckled. Her computer screen came to life with a series of clicks and clacks and pings. Every time she started the thing, she said a little prayer that it would keep working for awhile longer. She couldn't afford to buy a new one quite yet, although it was on her wish list. She started clicking icons to open the file she was after.

During the time Carson had been upstairs, Gracie had seriously contemplated the sanity of renting the shop and the apartment to him and his daughter. She'd had her doubts early on—then in a moment of stupidity had reconsidered. Now, she was sure she should not rent to him. Quite sure.

There was no sound reason why she shouldn't, really. He appeared to be a friendly person with good character and sincere intentions. He wasn't some derelict off the street. He was a family man with a child to raise. Besides, a nice cafe next door would certainly complement her shop.

The members of the Chamber would welcome the new business endeavor.

But she didn't know the wisdom of renting to this man who made her insides flutter. She wasn't used to fluttering insides and she didn't want them to flutter. She was just going to have to come up with some excuse *not* to rent to him.

*Tick. Tick. Tick.*

"Oh, shut up!"

"Excuse me?"

Startled, Gracie turned toward the voice. "Oh! Mr. Price."

"Were you talking to someone?" he asked with a slight smirk on his face. "I swear I heard you tell someone to shut up." He glanced about the shop. "And I don't see anyone else here but the two of us."

Gracie felt her cheeks grow warm with embarrassment. He was teasing her, and she wasn't sure she liked it. Or maybe, she liked it a little too much.

"I was—" She glanced around the shop. Where in the heck was that shop cat when she needed her? A lot of people talked to animals, didn't they? Then she glanced back at her computer. "I was . . . I was talking to the computer," she added quickly, then patted the monitor and turned back with a small grin. "I have to talk to her once in a while, a little sweet talk, you know. She works better for me that way."

"She?" Carson arched a brow in amusement.

Gracie wrung her hands and glanced off to the side. "Ah . . . yes. She. The computer is definitely a *she.*"

He nodded slowly, the expression on his face still resembling amusement. "But that didn't sound like sweet talk to me."

How in the heck was she going to talk her way

out of this one? Gracie cocked her head to one side. "Well . . . I'd be inclined to agree with you, Mr. Price, but—" She turned and patted the computer monitor again. "—you don't know old Clara Belle here. She needs a good swift, sweet-talking nudge once in a while."

As if on cue, the newly christened Clara Belle sputtered with another series of clicks and a bing as if she were acknowledging her own incompetence.

Gracie then arched her brow and looked once more to Carson. She shrugged. "See? What did I tell you?"

"Well, I fail to see—"

"So, how is Izzie?" She had to turn this conversation quickly. She had no intention of sharing with Carson Price the fact that she had these ongoing conversations with her biological clock.

"Oh, she's fine. All bandaged up and ready to move on to another escapade." He glanced back toward the stairwell. "She's actually staking claim on her room in the apartment upstairs. I hope you don't mind, but while we were up there, we went ahead and looked around."

Gracie was a bit taken aback. "Oh?" She remembered now that she had unlocked the apartment earlier this morning.

"Yes."

"And?"

"We love it."

"Oh."

"So, we'd like to take the package deal."

"You would?" Gracie wasn't sure whether to be thrilled or panicked.

"Yes. The apartment and the shop. I'd like to move as soon as possible, if that's okay with you. In fact, I'd like to start this weekend."

"But I have to clean—"

"No, forget about that. If you'll give me a cut on the first month's rent, I'll clean and even paint Izzie's bedroom upstairs. She wants purple. I hope you don't mind. She said pink was for girls. And I've claimed dibs on the blue room at the back, so the pink room has to go."

The blue room in the back. The room next to mine, Gracie thought. One thin wall separating us.

Oh, boy.

She took a deep breath. "Mr. Price. I think we need to discuss a few things before—"

"Do you have a lease?"

Puzzled, Gracie suddenly lost her train of thought. "Well, yes, I do. It's in the computer, in fact, but—" She wasn't sure she was ready to do this yet.

"Good. Why don't you print one off? I'll take it with me tonight, read it over, and then come back in the morning with either the signed copy or notes about issues we need to discuss."

"But you haven't filled out an application yet."

He nodded. "Well, print one of those off, too, and I'll bring it in the morning. You can sign the lease after you've checked my references."

"Well, I—"

Clara Belle clicked and pinged in the background again.

Carson chuckled and smiled at the machine. "I think she agrees. So, would you print all that off for me while I fetch Iz? I should be getting back to Louisville. We'll touch base in the morning then, if that's okay with you."

"Well, sure . . . I suppose. But—"

But he was gone, already moving toward the back of her shop. Gracie was at a loss for words.

Clara Belle pinged again. Gracie turned toward the computer and gave it one nasty look. "I didn't need your input back there a minute ago, you know. Whose side are you on, anyway?"

The computer monitor sat unmoving, silent.

"Oh hell," Gracie muttered quietly. Then she clicked on the program where she'd saved a copy of her standard lease and application, made a few impromptu adjustments, tweaked a couple of other items, and generally made some overall ridiculous changes. Maybe, once he'd looked this over, he would decide not to rent after all.

She sure hoped so. It would be much easier if he said no, rather than her having to say no to him. She didn't want him to get the wrong idea. She didn't want him to think that Izzie was the reason she couldn't rent to him.

In fact, she actually liked Izzie. She just couldn't see how she could live next to the child's father. Not when he made her insides flutter.

She printed off the lease and application then, not putting any further thought into it, and kept her fingers crossed that he would decide not to return with them in the morning.

# FOUR

Normally, after a day like today, Carson had little trouble dropping off to sleep. He'd run from one thing to another all day long; the trip to Franklinville and back, a meeting with a client, and a quick conference with Jack—all with Izzie in tow—which was, of course, a challenge. Always happiest when he was the busiest, though, he'd never had trouble with insomnia.

Until lately.

And tonight didn't seem to be an exception.

Lately, there had been one too many things on his mind; and it didn't matter how many sheep he counted or how many pages of some boring legal document he perused, sleep just sometimes didn't come.

Tonight was one of those nights.

Tonight, however, he wasn't thinking about Izzie and some problem at her school. He wasn't thinking about how Marci had all but abandoned her daughter three years ago—and now was making noises about coming back into his daughter's life. Nor was he thinking about the lucrative legal practice he was giving up to set up an "establishment" in the small burg of Franklinville.

No, none of those things entered his mind this night.

He was thinking about Gracie Hart. And why in the world she didn't want to rent to him.

Lying in his bed, a soft, cool breeze blowing over him from the window, Carson welcomed the night calm. Spring had finally arrived in Kentucky and he was thankful for the warm night and the soothing quiet it brought to the end of his day. The day had been rather hectic. He wished he could just let this calm wash over him totally and lull him to sleep.

With one arm thrown over his head and the other hand holding his copy of Gracie's lease, he squinted at the words while he read over the thing one more time by the dim light of his bedside lamp.

He couldn't figure out what she was up to. Unless it was just as simple as it looked: She didn't want to rent to him.

Period.

She'd jacked up the rent.

She'd made it impossible to do any physical alterations on the shop, including plumbing.

She'd essentially implicated that Izzie would have to leave her room pink.

She had required an outlandish deposit plus the first and last month's rent up front.

She was nuts if she thought he would go for this.

Carson dropped the lease and application on his night table with a flutter, punched his pillow once, then twice, rolled over, and closed his eyes to try to sleep.

He had no idea what Gracie Hart was up to, but there wasn't a damned thing he could do about it tonight.

Tomorrow. That's when he'd take care of it.

Tomorrow he would find out why Ms. Hart did not want to rent to him.

Eyes still closed, he started to drift off to sleep, but her image danced before him. It bugged the hell out of him.

There was some reason she didn't want him and Izzie around. Well, after this morning, he supposed he had a pretty good idea why. It was just that he thought she had *liked* Izzie. She'd smiled at her and didn't seem too upset about the cookies and the teapot and she'd even appeared forgiving about the damages.

Maybe he was reading her all wrong.

Maybe he'd just have to prove to her tomorrow that things could be different.

Every Saturday morning, like clockwork, they showed up for coffee and gossip. It had been that way for almost nine years. Constance Greenspoon had shown up first, coffee cup in hand, early one Saturday morning, wanting to know if she could sit a spell in Gracie's cozy corner and read the morning paper. Gracie had eagerly obliged. Romantically Yours had been in existence for several months at that point, and Gracie was still grieving over the move from New York and all that had happened there. She welcomed the older woman into her shop with open arms.

Constance, claiming her age as somewhere beyond sixty, was like a breath of fresh air for Gracie. They'd quickly become fast friends, and Gracie had needed fast friends at that point in her life. Constance had left that morning with a bottle of bath salts the younger woman had concocted; the next Saturday morning she was back with Mary White in tow, coffee cup in her hand, as well.

Evelyn Walters joined them the next week. Then Patsy Marcum. The next week Deni Carter.

And on it went.

The names and faces changed from time to time, year to year, but the camaraderie was still the same. Cait Conley had had twins in September and they hadn't seen much of her since. They'd lost Cassie Fields to cancer two years earlier and Sylvia Parker was beginning to suffer from Alzheimer's, but they weathered the storms just as they celebrated the joys.

It was what they were about. Life. Death. Living. Dying. And everything that came in between.

Coffee and gossip and the morning paper. Nothing more, nothing less. Constance often reported that they were worse than old men sitting around talking about old women.

And yes, the subject invariably turned to men, young or old. Short or tall, thin or fat. Straight or gay. Good-looking or not.

Gracie, the youngest of the bunch, kept quiet most of the time and listened, taking in the collective wisdom of the women who had grown to be her friends. There were times she welcomed their advice and their commonsense approach to life's trials and tribulations. There were other times she really didn't want to hear what they had to say.

Nevertheless, they'd been there for her when she'd needed a shoulder or two. Or three. Sometimes more.

It was the same most every Saturday morning, week in, week out. Year in, year out. And there was nothing different about this particular Saturday morning.

Except for the moment when Carson Price decided to grace her doorstep. Again.

The bell over the door chimed a warning at his entrance and Gracie sensed five pairs of eyes, in addition to hers, simultaneously look up and follow Carson as he crossed the shop's threshold and approached the group.

He stopped directly in front of Gracie, both feet firmly planted into the polished, hardwood floors. She looked up at him, her coffee cup poised halfway between the saucer and her mouth, and gulped.

*Oh damn. He's back.*

"I would like to talk to you, Ms. Hart, if you could spare a moment," he said to her then.

Gracie swallowed, looked into those eyes and held that connection for about three seconds, then slowly lifted the cup to her lips and took a sip as she glanced lower. She took her time with the sip and the following swallow, then turned her gaze back to Carson.

She was extremely proud of the self-control she exhibited.

Finally, she lowered cup and saucer to the table. "Of course, Mr. Price." She rose. "Right this way."

They'd walked perhaps two steps away, toward the cash register side of the shop, when Gracie heard the low buzz and chatter of the women behind her. She glanced back once and the babble stopped. When she turned to face Carson again, it resumed.

*Women.*

"I've come to talk to you about this lease," he began quietly.

Gracie glanced at the papers in his hand. "And?" she replied, looking back into his face. She wondered what kind of a poker face she possessed. It was hard being dead serious about the ridiculous lease she'd offered him. No one in town rented Main Street shops for that amount of money or required such a stiff deposit up front.

"It's absurd."

She already knew that.

"I'd like to discuss the terms."

She'd sort of figured that, too.

"I've done a little research around town and you're way out of line on the rent."

"Oh? Is that right?"

He arched a brow in disbelief and slowly nodded.

"Yes. And I've taken the liberty of redoing the lease with my acceptable offer to you. I'd like you to take a look at it; and if it's acceptable to you as well, I'd like to move some things into the apartment this afternoon."

Gracie stared at him. Then she chuckled. "Mr. Price, I think you are attempting to turn the table on me here."

He raised the other brow.

She continued, "I think it is customary, since I am the owner of the building, that I set the rent and the fees and the restrictions on the property, is it not?"

"Yes, ma'am, it is. However—"

"Then I'm sure you'll understand when I tell you that the lease, as originally written, stands. Nothing more, nothing less. Now, if you'll excuse me—"

She turned and started back toward the buzz growing louder in the rear of the shop. In an instant, she caught Constance's eye, noticed the horrified expression on her face, and the "no" signal she was flashing with her hands.

What in the world?

Carson Price laid a hand on her forearm and asked her to wait. Turning, she forgot Constance for a second and looked back into those damned sea-blue eyes.

"I don't understand," he told her.

Watching his face, Gracie felt a sudden pang. As if she'd done something morally and ethically wrong and the guilt was about to consume her. Carson's face was telling a story and she wasn't quite sure she wanted to hear it—but was almost certain that she was about to.

"I need this place, Ms. Hart. Please hear me out. I have no idea why you don't want to rent to me, but would you please just talk with me about this for a minute or two? Would you please just give me that?"

Gracie swallowed hard and searched Carson's face a little longer. Then for some reason, she glanced back at the women behind her. Smiling, Constance slowly nodded and gave her a thumb's up sign. The other four women nodded in unison beside her.

It was a conspiracy. Plain and simple.

"All right," she said. "Let's talk."

A commotion erupted behind her then and Gracie turned once more to see all five women standing, gathering their coffee cups and newspapers and purses. They were chatting about this and that, nodding and speaking their brief farewells as they passed.

Constance, in particular, had a huge grin plastered all over her face.

Not much later, after the doorbell chiming their departure silenced, Gracie found herself alone in her shop with Carson.

Finally, she motioned toward the corner the women had just left. "Would you like to sit down?"

He faltered a second, then agreed. "Sure."

Gracie followed him. He chose a Queen Anne wingback; she chose the overstuffed armchair opposite him. "Coffee? Tea?" She motioned toward the table between them.

He shook his head. "No, thank you."

"Pastry?"

"No."

"Cook—"

"Ms. Hart, why is it you don't want to rent to me?"

"Why Mr. Price, I've never said—"

"It's Izzie, isn't it?"

That thought had never entered her mind. Even though she was sure the child was a handful, Gracie thought her rather precious. No, the reason she didn't want to rent to him had nothing to do with his daughter; it had everything to do with Carson Price himself. "No," she told him.

"No?"

"No."

"Aha! Well then, if not Izzie, what is it?"

Clearing her throat, Gracie glanced about the shop. Reason. Suddenly her brain was all jumbled. What *was* the real reason she didn't want to rent to him? Let's see, there was one, wasn't there? Otherwise she wouldn't have jumped up the rent.

"Well?"

She looked into his eyes again. Oh damn, yes. That was it. Those eyes, and the man attached to them.

"Mr. Price, there is no reason not to rent to you. I've given you my terms. It's up to you to accept them or not." Gracie rose.

So did he.

"The terms are ridiculous and unacceptable."

"But they are my terms."

"All the more reason for me to believe that you have some ulterior motive for not wanting to rent to me. Did you get another offer? Is someone else actually going to rent from you for this exorbitant price? Because if there is—"

"No, Mr. Price. That's not it."

He threw his hands up in the air. "Then what is it?"

Heaving a thick sigh, Gracie turned away from him and walked toward her cash register. On the pretense of organizing her cash drawer, she gave herself a few seconds to settle her brain and organize her thoughts. She had to give him a reason; she had a feeling he wouldn't leave without one. But what in the world could she say? *I don't want to rent to you because you're too good-looking and you make my heart flutter?*

Somehow, she didn't think that would cut it.

"Well?"

She looked at him. He looked back, waiting for her to reply, appearing to study her face. "I've decided not to rent out that side of the building after all. The apartment, either." Where that statement came from, she had no clue. It was a weak reason. She knew it and so did he. Thing was, she couldn't back that up for long. She needed to rent out the whole shebang and soon. There were bills that needed to be paid.

Suddenly, he looked defeated. The hand that still held the lease dropped to his side and he glanced away. For a few seconds, she watched his profile as the expression there appeared to fall away, too. He heaved a sigh, his chest rising and then falling, and he exhaled long and slow. Finally, he turned back to fully face her.

"All right then. I suppose I have to accept that. Maybe I can find something else. It was just that this seemed so . . . perfect." His words were spoken with a hush that caught her totally off guard. There was something in his voice, some inflection that echoed something more than just mere disappointment. Something she couldn't quite put her finger on.

"Thanks for your time," he said then and turned to leave. "Sorry to interrupt your Saturday morning."

He set the papers on her counter and started for the door. Gracie watched his back as he moved away from her, his shoulders appearing to slump further with every step he took. In the next minute, he slowly opened the door and stepped out to the street.

An awful, empty feeling suddenly landed with a thud in the hollow place in Gracie's belly. She didn't like it.

"So, we're not moving to Franklinville?" Izzie looked up at him with confused eyes. Carson laid the storybook he'd been reading to her on his lap and gathered the child under his arm. Tucking the covers up around her, he hugged her tight. Darn it. He should have just kept quiet about his plans until everything was set. The child had gone through enough transitions in her life; she didn't need to endure more than necessary.

Lesson learned, Price. Next time keep it all under your hat until everything is squared away.

"Dad?" Her eyes were huge with question.

He took in a stabilizing breath. "No, Iz. I'm sorry to say, but that didn't work out."

"But I thought that's why you went back to see Ms. Hart today. To work out the deal."

"I did."

"But you didn't?"

He shook his head. "No, we didn't agree on a couple of things."

"But I liked . . . my room. I liked her."

The words stunned him. Studying his daughter's face, he took in the honest expression in her eyes. Izzie was a lot of things—mischievous, sneaky, and more often than not she carried around more than her share of assertiveness—but she was never dishonest with him. She always owned up to things and, to his knowledge, she never said things she didn't mean. For some reason, she had suddenly accepted this move. And for another, it seemed she honestly liked Grace Hart.

"Well, yeah, I know. I sort of liked her, too. And I really liked the shop and the apartment and the town. But the fact remains that the place was just too expensive for us and she wasn't willing to lower the rent."

"But did you try to talk to her?"

"I did."

"Did you talk to her real nice and sweet?"

He smiled. He hadn't, had he? Suddenly, he wondered if that would have worked.

No. It wouldn't have. Grace Hart was all business; he wouldn't have swayed her with sweet talk. In fact, she probably would have booted him right out on his ear had he tried.

"You didn't, did you, Dad?" She furrowed her

brow at him, pretending to be mad, but he saw right through her.

Smiling, he shook his head and ruffled her hair. "Nope, you little Munchkin, I guess I didn't. Think that would have helped?"

Izzie tilted her chin and tossed him a saucy little grin. "I bet you didn't do the eye thing, either, did you?"

This time she had him. "The eye thing?" he questioned.

"Yeah." She nodded. "You know, like when you talk to a pretty lady and you do that thing with your eyes."

Carson guffawed. "What! What thing do I do with my eyes?" Obviously, his daughter was a lot more observant than he'd realized.

"Oh, you know. You do like this." Izzie narrowed her eyes a bit, a sort of half-open, half-closed bedroomy eye thing, and arched one brow a bit. There was a little come-hither twinkle in the eye under that arched brow that took him totally by surprise.

Carson laughed out loud. "Izzie! I don't do that!"

"Oh yes, you do, Dad."

"Do not!"

"Do so!"

"Says who?"

"Says me!"

"I don't think—"

"The phone!" Izzie jumped up and scrambled out of the bed the instant the shrill ring sounded. She was gone in a flash and the eye thing was forgotten.

"Izzie! Let it go. Let the machine . . ."

But it was too late. He heard his daughter answer with an excited hello. God, how he hated this. Every time the phone rang late at night she rushed for it, thinking that it might be Marci. It rarely was. The California calls had been few and far between for the past couple of years.

Izzie returned to the bedroom with portable phone in hand and a disappointed face.

"For you, Dad."

He smiled at her and she shrugged, then handed over the phone. Slowly, she climbed back into bed.

He put the phone to his ear. "Hello?"

"Mr. Price?"

"Yes?"

"Grace Hart here."

He sat up, suddenly more interested in the call. "Yes?" he repeated. Izzie sat up, too, watching him and listening to his every word.

"I've been looking over your suggestions for the lease. I was wondering . . . perhaps we could talk about them."

For some reason, his heart started pounding. "Absolutely."

"Tomorrow?"

"Yes, of course."

"One o'clock?"

"That's fine."

"Please bring Isabella."

He nodded and then felt silly, knowing she couldn't see the nod. Suddenly, he was glad she couldn't see him, because he was smiling, very broadly. "Yes. She'll come, too."

"Wonderful."

"See you at one."

"I'll be there."

The phone clicked. Carson pushed the button to disconnect from his end. For a few seconds, he sat in disbelief of the brief conversation.

"Dad?" Izzie punched him and he smiled.

"Yes?"

"We're going back to Franklinville?"

"Yep."

"Are we happy about it?"

"Yep."

"Are we moving?"

"I think so."

"Good."

Izzie grinned, and for some crazy, silly reason, Carson joined her.

"Dad?" she queried again.

"Umhmmm?"

"You're doing that eye thing."

Gracie slowly placed the phone back on the hook and tried to quiet the small quivering in her heart. She still wasn't quite sure why she'd made that call. Something—she wasn't sure what—had nagged her the remainder of the day after Carson had left.

In fact, it had nagged her until she'd picked up the lease he'd altered and read it.

He'd offered her a fair deal. The rent was more

than she would have asked for in the first place, more than she'd gotten from the last tenant. He'd offered to clean up both places, do a little repair work, paint, and make all alterations to the building and apartment under her guidance. He would do nothing without consulting her first. He offered a fair deposit up front, a year's lease, and would pay all utilities and deposits.

What more could she ask for? It was all too perfect. The dream tenant come true.

She'd thought long and hard about it and finally had concluded that this was a deal she could not pass up. Fluttering or no fluttering. The town could use another cafe, and she was happy that one would be located next to her shop. It would do wonders for her business. Actually, the two businesses would wonderfully complement each other. The Downtown Business Association would be delighted.

But besides all that, she was ecstatic that she was finally going to have income from the rental again.

That had been too long in coming.

There was nothing to do but take his offer. That's why she'd made the call.

That was the *only* reason she had made the call.

It was a business reason, pure and simple.

She was just going to have to keep that in mind. And she was just going to have to stand her ground about that fluttering-of-the-heart thing.

# FIVE

"Deal?"

"Deal."

"Deal!"

Izzie was the one to seal the deal with that final exclamation. Carson grinned at his daughter, then put his hand out to shake Gracie's. He watched her eyes as she hesitantly thrust her hand forward, gripped and shook his hand very quickly, then dropped her arm to her side.

Her hesitancy bothered him a bit. Was she still reluctant to rent to him or did something else concern her? There was something there, something he couldn't quite put his finger on.

Her hand was warm, soft, and much smaller than his. Her fingers were long and graceful, just like the rest of her; and it seemed, for the brief second they'd touched his, they had wrapped around his hand in one fluid movement. He almost didn't want to let her go. In fact, he wouldn't have minded at all if she'd let her hand linger a bit longer so he could lightly caress her softness.

But she let go much too quickly and he dismissed the direction of his thoughts.

"Mr. Price, it looks as if you've got yourself a cafe."

Stunned at the sound of that, Carson's thoughts immediately shot back to his purpose for renting the shop and apartment in the first place. The sudden insight that his goal was about to become reality was almost startling. "Well, yes, I suppose I do," he said sheepishly, then glanced to Izzie. "That's right, hey, Munchkin?" He winked at her, hoping she would take the hint and not spill the beans.

Izzie winked back. Carson sighed.

"So, tell me, Mr. Price," Gracie continued, "will this be just a soup-and-sandwich kind of place or more than that?"

This Mr. Price stuff was getting to him. "*Carson.* It's *Carson.* I'm leaving Mr. Price back in Louisville," he told her. "If you don't mind."

Gracie dipped her head in a slow nod, her eyes playing over his face. "Oh! Well, of course. Carson."

"Good."

He could tell she was thinking about that. "If you don't mind my asking, Carson, may I inquire as to what *is* the "Mr. Price" profession you are leaving back there in Louisville?"

"Attorney," he answered quickly. Then he decided to go on with his usual disclaimer. "I'm tired of the rat race, the long days, and the hours spent away from Izzie. It's time for a life change. This appears to be it."

"And the cafe?" she queried again.

"Yes, the cafe."

"More than soup and sandwich?" she asked again.

"Umm . . . yeah. More than a soup-and-sandwich place," he told her.

"Dinner?"

He nodded. "Oh, yes. Dinner, too."

"How lovely! We need a nice dinner cafe around here. All the cafes on Main Street are open only for lunch right now. Having someplace for dinner will be nice. In fact . . ."

Carson watched her gaze drift off to the side. He could literally see the wheels inside that pretty head of hers turning. Damn.

". . . you know, I might even consider staying open late an evening or two, in case some of your dinner customers would wander by."

Hell. He felt like a heel and he didn't want to talk about his "cafe" plans any longer, lest he let something slip. Or heaven forbid, Izzie let something slip. He shouldn't have clued her in on all the plans yet for Geekmeister's CyberCafe. But he'd thought it such a neat idea, he'd just had to share it with Izzie last night.

He supposed bar food could constitute dinner. And he supposed video computer games and a big screen TV for sporting events could count as "more than a soup-and-sandwich place." So, he really wasn't lying, was he?

He didn't want to stick around any longer than necessary to contemplate that thought.

It was time to give Gracie the check for the deposit, let her bank it, and get this show on the road.

He'd feel a whole lot better when all that was done and a few days had passed.

He cleared his throat and reached into his back pocket for his checkbook. She glanced back to him.

"Well, I'll have to think about that, " she said.

She was talking about her late hours. "Yes, you do that." God, he hated deceiving her, if one could actually call this deceit. Really, though, his crime was nothing more than just letting her *assume* his plans. He'd never really indicated otherwise.

"Please let me know your plans about moving and such," she said, bringing him back to the moment at hand, "and I'll make sure the apartment is cleaned."

"Oh, but we'll do that. You don't have to."

She shook her head. "No, I insist. It will be easier to clean now than after you've moved things in. I'll have a service come in tomorrow morning."

He nodded. "Well, all right. Actually, I was thinking of taking next week off to do whatever is necessary about getting the place livable. You know, get the utilities turned back on, paint Izzie's room . . ."

"The utilities are already turned on," she told him. "All you have to do is have the accounts transferred into your name."

Carson liked the sound of that. "So, we could actually move in tonight?" He was already thinking sleeping bags and camping out on the living room floor. His brain was reeling. He could get Izzie registered in school and get started on their new life.

"I suppose, but—"

"Then that's what we'll do." Glancing at his

watch, he mentally calculated how much time was left in the day to get to Louisville, gather what they'd need for a day or two, and get back here tonight. No time like the present to get started on his new life. He was deep in thought when he realized Gracie was talking to him again.

". . . but I wouldn't feel comfortable knowing that you were moving in with the place still dirty. And where would Izzie sleep? Of course, I suppose she could stay in my spare room if you wanted, and you—"

Her eyes grew wide and she abruptly snapped her mouth shut.

"We have sleeping bags," he told her.

"Oh." She paused. "But I'm not sure how comfortable those hardwood floors—"

"We'll be fine."

"Are you sure you want to move tonight? I mean—"

Carson held up a hand. "Wait." Flipping open his checkbook, he took a minute to write out a check, carefully tore it from the book, and handed it to her. "Here is the deposit and the first month's rent. Now the place is officially mine, right? I'm moving in later tonight. If you want the cleaning service to come first thing in the morning, that will be fine. Until then, Izzie and I can fend for ourselves." He glanced to the child. "Actually, we're used to a little dust, aren't we, Iz?"

Izzie nodded furiously. "Actually, sometimes we're used to a lot of—"

"Enough, Iz." Carson chuckled. "Ms. Hart might

kick us out on our ears if she thinks we're not good tenants."

Izzie clamped her mouth shut and made a funny face. Carson had to laugh out loud. Looking to Gracie, he also noticed she was smiling, intent on Izzie's antics. He took in that smile for a moment and let himself wonder just a little bit more about Gracie Hart. What was her story? Why *didn't* she have a ring on the third finger of her left hand? He mentally chastised himself for noticing.

"Well, I'll let you in on a little secret, Izzie," she said as she leaned closer to the girl, interrupting his thoughts. "Sometimes I have a little too much dust in my house, too."

Izzie giggled, her big eyes animated. "Betcha don't have as much as us! One time, me and Dad wrote our entire whole names in the dust on the bookshelves and it stayed that way for weeks!"

"Izzie!"

"Well, it did!"

"Did not."

"Did so!"

"Well, okay. You could be right. But you know you're not supposed to tell those things!"

Gracie laughed again, and for the second time that afternoon, Carson found himself mesmerized by her smile and captivated by the sound of her laugh—and very curious as to what made Gracie Hart tick.

\* \* \*

"Okay, Gracie, spill it about the new guy next door."

Amie, always on the lookout for new guys in town, chewed on a blueberry bagel and looked across the table at Gracie, staring her square in the eye. "You've been holding out on me. I hear he's a doll."

Gracie snorted and took another sip of hot lemon tea. "A doll? Hardly." If it were up to *her* to find words to describe Carson Price, *doll* would not be on the list. *Hunk? Stud puppy?* Those two descriptive terms came to mind quite quickly, and if pressed, Gracie was sure she could drum up a few more. Yes, he was a very attractive man. Of course, she wasn't the least bit interested in drumming up descriptive terms for the likes of Carson Price—or any man, for that matter.

She was only interested in Carson Price for his rent check, although it seemed her friends had other thoughts on the subject.

*Nice-looking eligible bachelor* were the words Constance had thrown up to her the day before. Gracie had shushed her off with a wave of her hand. Gracie Hart wasn't on the lookout for nice-looking eligible bachelors, she'd told Constance.

The older woman had made some comment, but Gracie had pretended not to hear. Something about specific parts of her anatomy shriveling up from lack of use . . .

"You know he's the talk of the town." Amie interrupted her thoughts. "I mean, all the women have been sneaking by to peek in the window at him. I haven't had the chance. So, spill."

Fiddling with her teacup, Gracie stared off into Amie's coffee shop, trying not to think about atrophying body parts. It was early Friday morning, two hours before her shop and most of the others on Main Street opened for the day. The coffee shop was on the same side of the street as Romantically Yours, but on the other side of the traffic light. She was North Main, Amie was South Main. About a dozen people were occupying space with them, drinking tea or coffee and eating bagels and pastries.

Amie's Place, which also served a light lunch, closed at two in the afternoon. That's the way Amie liked it. She had the remainder of the day to play.

Gracie already knew Carson was the talk of the town. Her own business had been booming for the past few days since he'd moved in and started some minor renovations. The talk from the women was nonstop. Gracie would smile and nod and try not to get drawn into the middle of those oh-God-he's-so-gorgeous conversations.

She'd talked to him only once, and briefly at that, during the week. Seems his plans were to open his cafe at the end of the month, barely three weeks away. Izzie, she'd learned, was staying in Louisville for the next two weeks with her baby-sitter until school was out for the summer. Then she would be joining her father. For some reason, Gracie had felt a sense of urgency from Carson that he get the cafe up and running as soon as possible. She wondered what that urgency was all about.

She supposed he was just ready to get on with his

new life. Of all people, she could understand that. Once upon a time, she'd done the same thing.

But she tried not to think about that much anymore. Ten years was a long time, but she was proud of the way she had recovered.

"Of course, *you* wouldn't sneak a peek, would you, Gracie?"

Had Amie said something? Grace's thoughts were temporarily back in New York. Gracie looked at her and said, "I'm sorry. You were saying?"

Amie huffed. "I said, you wouldn't sneak a peek, would you?"

*"Moi?* Of course not." New York was all but forgotten.

"Yeah, right."

"Well, I, for one," Gracie returned, "have more things to do with my time than ogle my next-door neighbor while he hammers two-by-fours and moves equipment about, wearing nothing more than a pair of tight jeans and work boots, perspiration glistening off his back like some model in a diet soft drink commercial."

"So, you've never even peeked, huh?"

Gracie shook her head. "Nope, not interested."

Amie snorted and then laughed out loud. About six customers turned to look at her. "Like I said, yeah, right."

Gracie stuck out her tongue at her friend and picked up her cinnamon bagel. "You're impossible."

"And you're lying. I know you, Gracie Hart. There is something up with this man."

"You're wrong." Grace bit off a bite of bagel,

looked Amie square in the eye. "There is . . . nothing up . . . with that man," she returned between chews.

Sitting back in her seat and pushing her coffee cup away at the same time, Amie crossed her arms over her chest. Gracie didn't like the way she was studying her. "Well, I'll tell you what. I'll reserve comment on that subject until a later date. Until I have some time to see you around this man. I mean, Constance told me the other day—"

"Constance?" Gracie sat up a little straighter. "What does Constance have to do with this conversation?" Knowing that Constance and Amie had been talking made Gracie uncomfortable. Even though the two women were her friends and had good intentions, she didn't want them joining forces *again* to instigate something into an area of her life where Gracie had no intention of going.

Would those two never stop trying to hook her up with a man?

"Oh, nothing," Amie replied, popping the last bite of bagel into her mouth. "You know, Gracie, I am a bit miffed at you, however."

Puzzled, Gracie stared at her friend. "Whatever for?"

"Allowing him to come into town and open up another cafe. I mean, when the soup-and-sandwich place closed down the street, I all but had a monopoly on the lunch crowd."

"My goodness, you *have* the monopoly on the breakfast crowd! And more customers than you can handle, as I recall, at lunch," Gracie told her.

"Weren't you just complaining last week that you weren't prepared for the onslaught and that people could barely get in the door during their lunch hour?"

"Complaining? No. Drooling at the thought of the increase in lunch sales? Yes. But now I suppose—"

Leaning forward, Gracie replied, "Look, Amie. Carson Price's putting in another cafe down the street is not going to ruin your business. If lunch customers can't get in your door because it's too crowded and the service is slow, do you think they are going to come back? No. And besides, Carson's place is going to be different from yours, not just a soup-and-sandwich place, he said. In fact, he's even going to be open for dinner."

Amie thought about that. "Not just a soup-and-sandwich place, huh? Wonder what he meant by that?"

Gracie shrugged. "Not sure. I just think he must be designing something fairly upscale since he's planning to be open for dinner, too." Her thoughts drifted for a moment, then she looked at Amie. "I wonder . . . wouldn't it be great if he were putting in some sort of tea room? I mean, that would be so cool right next door. We could possibly double up on advertising and marketing and bring in customers for each other . . ."

Thoughts were swimming in her head. This could be perfect. This could be just the thing she needed. She couldn't wait until the next meeting of the Chamber.

"I dunno," her friend said. "Carson Price doesn't look much like the tea room type to me."

But Gracie wasn't listening. Visions of increased business and new customers were dancing in her head.

Amie touched her arm.

"What?"

"I said why don't you ask him now."

Gracie shook her head. "Excuse me?"

Pointing with her thumb over her shoulder, Amie directed Gracie's attention to the front of the shop. "That's him, right? Why don't you go discuss business with him now? See if you two could drum up some *business* together."

Gracie sucked in a deep breath. Amie's innuendo stood for more than business, she knew. Turning, she looked in the direction her friend pointed. There he stood at the front counter—wearing tight jeans, work boots, and a black t-shirt that fit like a second skin—ordering breakfast to go.

"Doesn't look like any lawyer I ever met," Gracie muttered.

"What?"

She sat up straighter and looked at Amie. "Wait a minute. You said you'd never seen him. How did you know that was Carson Price up there?"

Amie tossed her an evil little grin and tilted her chin a bit. "Oh, all right. So, I lied. I peeked. And, oh yeah, he comes in here every morning for breakfast. Just in case you'd like to know."

Amie grinned wide and giggled and Gracie could

all but strangle her. She was up to something. So was Constance. And that didn't bode well for her.

"Just a large coffee, black, and one of those honey buns. To go."

Carson eyed the young girl across the counter as she turned and headed for the coffeemaker. She couldn't be more than seventeen, he thought. Yet, she was ogling him and smiling as if he were prime rib.

Another teenager sidled up next to her, pretending to get coffee as well. She glanced back at him and both girls giggled. He thought he heard one of them say something about "his honey buns" and tried like hell to ignore that statement.

Briefly, he closed his eyes and shook his head. It had been like this all week. If it wasn't the two teenagers behind the counter who served him breakfast every morning, it was the same group of women who sauntered by his place every afternoon as though they were window-shopping. Sighing, he glanced around the shop. His gaze immediately lit on a tall blonde in the back of the room.

*Gracie?*

"Honey bun . . . and coffee."

He turned back to the girl. She set his coffee and pastry down on the counter with a sassy seventeen-year-old smile and stared at him while he produced the couple of dollar bills and the change he owed her.

What was it with this town? Ever since Tuesday

women had been parading by his windows, staring as if they'd never seen a man before.

*New man in town. Single. Eligible bachelor.*

*Oh, hell.*

Out of the blue, the concept hit him square in the face. He didn't like it. Old memories festered up mighty quickly and he shook himself, desperately trying to tamp them down.

Living in Louisville for the past twenty years, he'd forgotten about small town antics. He should have known. He'd grown up in a little village just east of Cincinnati where everyone knew everyone else and no one thought twice about getting involved in their neighbor's business. That was one of the reasons he had preferred the city. One could get lost in the shuffle and do his own thing and not worry about what his neighbor thought or did. It just had never occurred to him that he would have to revert back to dealing with small town antics here in Franklinville.

It was the one thing he'd forgotten.

He hoped he could at least avoid the gossips, busybodies, and matchmakers. He'd had enough of that growing up. If there were anything he disliked more, he didn't know what it would be.

"Get you anything else?" The teenager batted her eyes.

"No. No thank you," he told her.

He risked a quick glance back to Gracie again. Yes, it was she. Just as quickly, she averted her gaze.

For some reason, that bothered him.

Gathering up his breakfast, he headed for the

door, wondering why she'd kept to herself all week. Then again, he'd not ventured far from his little corner of the world, either, had he? He'd thought, at the very least, she might be curious as to the renovations. Obviously, she wasn't, which was all the better for him.

"Oh, Mr. Price?"

*Gracie?*

No. It wasn't her voice. For some reason, though, he wanted it to be. Stopping, he turned to look behind him.

The woman who owned the coffee shop stood about three feet away. He'd not met her, but he knew who she was. He'd seen her here every morning and figured she was the "Amie" of Amie's Place. She commanded the most authority and was definitely the one in control. He'd also seen her at Gracie's once or twice and assumed they were friends.

She stepped closer. "If you're not in too much hurry, why don't you join us for breakfast?" She glanced back to Gracie. Carson followed her gaze and Gracie finally gave him a feeble smile and a little finger wave. She looked embarrassed.

It was a small smile. Almost an insecure little half-grin. And it intrigued the hell out of him.

Turning back to Amie he said, "I should really get down the street and to work."

But Amie was not about to take no for an answer. In one motion, she slipped her arm through his and led him toward the back of the coffee shop. "Oh c'mon, just for a few minutes," she told him. "Have a seat and savor that honey bun and coffee. Besides,

I can't give you free refills down the street, and if you stay, you can take one to go when you leave."

Well, she was right about that. Before he knew it, he was sitting between Gracie and Amie.

There were a few awkward seconds between sips of coffee and tea before Gracie finally spoke.

"So, how are things coming along next door?"

Carson took another sip of coffee and finished chewing a bit of pastry. "Fine. Right on schedule." He nodded in acknowledgment of his own words and finished chewing at the same time.

"That's great," she added.

He dropped his head in another nod. "Actually, we're a little ahead of schedule. Besides the plumbing, there wasn't that much that required a lot of time. We'll definitely open before the end of the month."

Gracie nodded. "So, Carson. Can you tell us exactly what your cafe is going to be like? I mean, you've not really mentioned what your plans are."

For the first time that morning, Carson allowed his gaze to linger over Gracie's face. She appeared tense and nervous, almost as if she didn't want to be there. Or that she didn't want him to be there. Her gaze kept skittering away from his whenever he tried to make eye contact, while her fingers fiddled with the handle of her teacup.

Did he make her nervous?

Turning to his right, he took in the opposite expression on Amie's face. Her eyes appeared to twinkle, as if she were holding in a deep belly laugh and the tickle of it was about to make her explode.

Amie leaned forward. "We'd love to hear what you have in mind for the most recent addition to Main Street, Franklinville, Carson."

Oh hell, this one is going to call for fast thinking on your feet, old boy, Carson told himself. Reverting back to tactics he often used in the courtroom, Carson turned to Gracie. He felt certain he could dupe her more easily than he could dupe Amie. That one was a mite too precocious for her own good. Not that Gracie wasn't an intelligent woman; he was sure she was. There was just something that told him that Amie might be on to him more than Gracie was.

"I have a plan in mind," he started, "but it's sort of evolving as I go along. Things are coming to me as I work and, quite honestly, I think I'd like to keep most of them under my hat until the grand opening."

"Oooohhh, a man who likes a mystery," Amie chided. "He's going to keep us in suspense, Gracie."

Gracie studied him for a moment with a look he was quite certain he'd never seen on her face before. Suddenly, he wasn't sure if Amie was the one he needed to be concerned about.

"I'm sure Carson will let us in on his little secret in due time," she said, a matter-of-fact tone in her voice.

Then Amie spoke, glancing back and forth from Gracie to him, smiling all the while. "You know, there is a Chamber of Commerce luncheon next week, right Gracie? Perhaps Carson should come and introduce himself to the other business persons in the community and give us some small dribble of news about his new business venture. Would that be possible by then, Mr. Mystery Man?"

Carson stared at her for a moment. Just what was Amie getting at? She *did* know something, didn't she? No, impossible. He was just being paranoid. The only persons who knew about his real plans for the cafe were Izzie and his brother. Her suggestion wasn't a bad idea, though. Besides being breeding grounds for gossips and busybodies, small towns were generally political towns; and networking with local business and professional organizations was exactly what he needed to be doing right now. He needed as many people on his side as he could get, especially when Gracie found out that he had actually duped her.

A small dribbling of information about his new business venture might actually be a good thing.

Funny, each time he thought about that, the guilt ate at him a little more.

"Sounds like a good idea to me," he replied. Then he turned to Gracie and looked her square in the eyes. "What do you think?"

She swallowed and stared back at him with wide eyes. "I . . . well, of course . . . I think it's great idea. As president of the Chamber, I think all businesses should belong. Amie and I are both active members."

Her words were much too stiff, forced, and contrived for his liking. Why couldn't he figure this woman out?

She motioned across the table then. "You *do* know

Amie, don't you? She owns the coffee shop. Amie Clarke, Carson Price."

Carson reached to his right and took Amie's hand. "I don't think we've officially met, but I've seen you here."

Amie gave him a firm handshake and a broad smile. "Yes, I've seen you, too. Nice to meet you, Carson. And welcome to Franklinville. I'm sure you'll like it. We're small town, middle America, at its best. Home of nosey neighbors, troublesome busybodies, and matchmakers. Make yourself at home."

It was all Carson could do not to spit his last sip of coffee straight across the table. And it would have been an understatement to say that he was totally taken off guard when Gracie did exactly that.

# SIX

Izzie arrived with a flourish and a grin and a small, yappy puppy early on a Sunday morning. Or at least, that's when she made her presence known. The child could have arrived the night before for all Gracie knew. Yawning, she pulled the covers back over her head. This was her morning to sleep in, to unwind, to read the paper in bed and allow her brain unravel.

Sunday was her day to spoil herself.

Sometimes, she'd light candles and burn incense and drink a glass of white zin while she soaked the afternoon away in her antique clawfoot tub.

Other days, she'd indulge herself in sappy movies and chocolate ice cream while staying in her jammies all day long.

Once in a while she'd engross herself in some long-forgotten artsy-crafty project just to get her mind off the shop.

Today, she just wanted to sleep. That was the only thing on her agenda. Amie had treated her to margaritas and fajitas at her house the night before, and

Gracie felt slightly hungover this morning. A rare occurrence, but nonetheless, very real.

This particular Sunday morning, however, didn't appear to be one destined for a pampering ritual.

Small, running footsteps, up and down the back stairs, echoing inside her head with every thump . . . thump . . . thump, came first. Those were followed closely by shrieks and shouts. Then a giggle or two. Mixed throughout were yips and yaps and sometimes even a feisty little puppy growl.

The dog's name was *Bandit,* she'd also learned. Izzie had screamed the pup's name every time it yipped and growled.

Gracie searched her fuzzy little brain. Had she put anything in the lease about pets?

Damn. She couldn't remember.

She pulled her covers up tighter over her ears. She'd managed for two weeks to avoid Carson and she really didn't want to approach him first thing this morning. Certainly, she could just ignore the child and the dog, stuff some imaginary cotton in her ears and go back to sleep—

"Bandit, *no!*"

"Yip! Yip!"

"Eeeek!"

*Stomp. Stomp. Stomp.*

"Izzie! Quiet that pup down!"

That last shout was from Carson.

How quickly the two weeks had passed. It seemed only yesterday that she had embarrassed herself to no end when Amie made that crack about busybodies and matchmakers. Along with the covers, Gracie pulled her pillow over her head and grimaced, still embarrassed at the thought of her spitting tea across the table all over Carson.

How stupidly embarrassing.

She'd not faced the man since.

And no matter what, she didn't plan on facing him this morning.

Ahhh . . . silence. Blessed silence.

Gracie inhaled deeply, then let out a relaxed sigh. Carson must have commandeered the child and the pup to another location.

"Thank you," she whispered as she felt herself drifting again.

Then she heard: *Eeeeeeeeeek! Yip! Yip! Yip! Me-OWWWWW!* And a loud tumbling and rumbling that echoed down the stairwell mingled with a small whine, a puppy whimper, a final shriek, and a sob.

Silence.

*"Izzie!"*

That was Carson.

More silence. Then heavy footsteps.

Gracie sat straight up in bed. Izzie had fallen down the stairs! The dog! The cat?

She leapt from her bed and took off toward the door with no regard to the fact that she didn't want to see Carson or that she probably looked like hell or that she was wearing nothing more than an over-sized t-shirt and black bikini panties.

Jerking open the door leading directly to the stairway landing, Gracie bolted smack into Carson. She shrieked and each of them scrambled and sidetracked the other and made apologies and some sort of incoherent babble, then raced to the bottom of the stairs.

"Izzie! Oh my God!"

Gracie wasn't sure if those were her words or Carson's.

They lay in a pile at the foot of the steps, the pup and the girl. The pup was whining. The cat was nowhere to be found. The girl was sobbing softly—big, fat tears sliding down her face as she looked up at the two adults barreling down the stairs toward her. Izzie held the tiny Bandit in her hands.

"I smashed her!" she sobbed loudly. A look of horror lanced across her face.

"Let me see," Carson told her softly, reaching for the pup. He did a quick inspection. Bandit nipped at his finger, and he proclaimed her okay.

Gracie breathed a small sigh. If Izzie were more worried about the pup than herself, she was probably okay. Carson gathered both child and dog into his arms and pulled them closer. She noticed he was doing a quick inspection of his daughter as well, running his hands over her arms and legs, checking for injuries.

"Izzie," he breathed, "you scared the heck out of me."

Gracie realized her own heart was beating mighty quickly as she watched Carson sit on the bottom step and cradle his daughter and her puppy closer. She placed a hand over her heart and willed it to stop beating so wildly. Carson's eyes closed as he stroked the girl's hair and placed a light kiss on top of her head, his strong arms wrapped securely about her.

Finally, her heart slowed a bit.

"Are you okay, Munchkin?" Carson whispered to Izzie.

She sniffed and nodded. "B-Bandit—"

Carson cradled the tiny pup in his hand. The pup nuzzled under his chin. "She's fine."

Izzie sobbed again. "I didn't mean to fall on her."

"I know, honey."

"My . . . my feet got tangled . . . around her . . . and the kitty . . . and I tripped and . . ." she said between sniffs.

"She's okay, Munchkin," Carson assured her.

Izzie looked up at her father. "You're sure?"

As if on cue, Bandit barked.

Carson nodded. "See, she's fine."

"What about the kitty?"

"I'm sure she's fine, too." Carson glanced around. Still no kitty. Gracie figured Claire had skedaddled at the first inkling of disaster. She wasn't worried. Claire was a cat who could take care of herself.

Izzie took the pup away from him. "Bad puppy," she told the dog. "You have to stay out from under my feet."

Carson grasped Izzie's chin and turned her face so she would look at him. "Iz, I told you not to run on the stairs. You . . . and the pup . . . could have been hurt very badly."

Izzie cradled the puppy closer. "I know. Sorry."

Gracie heard Carson sigh and sensed his relief. After a moment, he glanced up. At that precise sec-

ond Gracie realized she wasn't an unobserved by-
stander to the situation any longer. It probably had
something to do with the way Carson's eyes grew
larger as his gaze traveled slowly from her painted
toenails up to her face.

She glanced down.

*Oh, no . . .*

Her heart started that wild beat again.

There was a moment, which seemed aeons ago
now, that Carson had registered running into Gracie
out in the hallway. Briefly, he recalled their bodies
bumping together and their exchanging a couple of
excited words as they raced down the stairway toward Izzie. After that, he'd lost track of her.

But she was a hard sight to lose track of at this
particular moment in time.

His mouth went suddenly dry and he swallowed.
Hard. He knew Grace was tall, but as she stood before him, she seemed nothing but legs. Long,
shapely legs. Dancer's legs, he'd heard them called.
And the big t-shirt she wore, which hit her about
midthigh, really wasn't doing its job of effectively
covering them.

But he guessed it wasn't meant to do that. Obviously, Gracie had just been roused from her bed.
He'd come to that conclusion as his gazed traveled
upward over her body. The shirt she wore was clearly
a nightshirt. Her rich blonde tresses lay long and
loose around her shoulders, unbrushed and un-

tamed. She wore no makeup, her face fresh and dewy, her eyes a little swollen from sleep.

From out of the blue he thought of Marci and how he'd loved the way she looked first thing in the morning, before she'd taken her shower and made herself up for the day. That was when he'd loved making love to her most.

But that was over three years ago. And making love with Marci was the furthest thing from his mind at the moment. In fact, the woman standing before him with the startled, doe-eyed look on her face was doing more things to his body than any other woman had in quite some time.

He stood, lifting Izzie off his lap. "Munchkin, why don't you take Bandit upstairs. I'll be along in a minute." He said the words to his daughter, realizing he'd not yet taken his eyes off Gracie.

For once Izzie minded him without protest and scooted up the stairs. He sent up a silent prayer.

"Uhhhhh . . ." Gracie started.

"About the pup," Carson began.

"It's okay. She can have her," Gracie intercepted.

"Well, there wasn't anything in the lease about pets. I wasn't sure. Was going to ask you today. We got in late last night."

Gracie took one step up the stairway. She pulled at her shirt, as if she were trying to make it longer, then crossed her arms over her chest. Didn't she realize that made it shorter?

"It's okay. As long as she's careful on the stairs. I think my heart is still in my throat." She smiled hesitantly, then took another step up and stopped.

"Well . . . I should be getting back upstairs . . . to my apartment."

She started to move up another step, clutched at her t-shirt again, then cautiously turned back to look at him. "Ummmm . . . would you mind going first?"

Carson then realized the reason for her wavering, of her not wanting to precede him up the stairway. From the lower position, he would have had a very nice view of her backside. And she knew it.

"Oh! Of course." *Idiot!* Carson mentally slapped himself on the forehead and moved upward, carefully moving past her. Not stopping, he ascended all the stairs until he reached the landing and the door to his apartment a few steps beyond. He laid a hand on his doorknob then risked a glance backward.

Gracie stood not six feet away, her hand on her doorknob, her head turning back to glance at him at the same time. Then at once, they both twisted their separate doorknobs and pushed their respective doors to the inside.

"Oh!"

"One more thing."

They spoke simultaneously.

Carson grinned. Gracie giggled.

"You first," she said.

"No, you," he returned.

Gracie bit her lip. Carson thought it was a cute gesture and not one he expected from Grace Hart, the businesswoman. Yet, Grace Hart the businesswoman was not standing before him at the moment. The woman standing before him was someone else . . . was simply, Gracie.

"Was just going to say," she began. "Well . . . was just going to apologize again to you for that tea-spitting thing the other day."

Carson gestured with his hand, reminded of the last time he'd seen her. "No problem. I understand. Anyone could choke on a bagel."

She smiled again. Lord save him. He liked that smile.

"You were going to say?" she asked then.

Nodding, Carson continued. I was just going to apologize for the pup. I should have asked first."

This time Gracie gestured with her hand. "Not a problem. With the pup, I mean." She turned to head into her apartment, then stopped and faced him once again. "Just don't make a habit of not asking, Mr. Price."

For a moment, he thought she was dead serious. Then he saw that smile return to her face and knew that she was teasing him.


With her back to her closed door, Gracie clamped her hands over her eyes and groaned. "Now what in the world did I go and do that for?" she chided herself.

Stepping away, she headed toward her bedroom and the sanctuary of her comfy bed. "My God, Gracie, you were flirting with him! Half-dressed, no less! Have you gone mad?"

Falling into her bed, she jerked the covers up to her neck, closed her eyes, and tried to erase the image of Carson standing before her at his apartment door. She tried not to think about the fact that the man had signed a year's lease and that he would be coming and going out of that door for months to come.

Oh my. What in the world would she do?

Opening her eyes wide again, she stared across the bedroom, letting her brain mull the situation.

Nothing. She would do nothing.

After all, there was nothing *to* do. She would just go about her daily routine, living her life, just as she had done for ten years now.

But the ticking started in her brain again and this time it appeared to be piercing her heart with every *tick, tick, tick* it drummed up.

"One of these days, Gracie Hart," she whispered to herself, "you're going to have to come face-to-face with your fears; do you know that?"

And she knew exactly what her fears were. Facing them was just the thing she had to learn to do. For some reason, she knew that day was coming closer. It had been ten years since she'd lost everything. Ten years since the accident, which took from her everything she'd ever loved—her fiancé and her dancing career.

Ten long, and sometimes lonely, years.

She never thought she'd end up like this: thirty-five, single, and childless—but this was her life. And now, an interesting man next door was making her heart flutter. A man who might even be a very nice candidate for someone to love.

She just didn't know if she could ever get over her fear about falling in love. Actually, it wasn't the

falling in love part that scared her so much—it was
losing that love that scared the hell out of her.


Later that evening, Carson glanced about the inside of Geekmeister's, not believing that the time
had almost come. The place had truly been trans-
formed. Three weeks of hard work and late nights
and his cafe was nearly up and running. He'd been
thinking how he would handle his grand opening,
debating whether to throw one hopping shindig of
a kickoff party or just quietly open his doors one
evening and see what happened. Maybe he'd host a
small party with some of his Louisville friends on
Friday night, a little live music, food and drink, and
just take it from there.

Since that was the direction he seemed to be leaning, Carson figured he probably needed to get himself in gear and start inviting people. Goodness
knows his friends loved their weekends and a good
party to boot. Well, they had best make time for him
on this particular Friday night.

It was high time Main Street, Franklinville, started
hopping. He chuckled at the thought.

Stepping closer to the front of the cafe, he stared
out the window to the dark, empty street lit with the
red glow of the traffic light and a smattering of
streetlights. Quiet, quaint little town. He liked it, but
it was a far cry from downtown Louisville, where
he'd lived since college.

He almost felt guilty thinking about how he was
going to break this calm next weekend. Of course,

today was Sunday and the town was cozily tucked in for the night, preparing for the work week. Friday and Saturday evenings were usually a little livelier.

It had crossed his mind that he should extend an invitation to Gracie. Maybe . . . just maybe . . . he should. On the one hand, there was no use borrowing trouble. On the other, he wouldn't be able to hide it from her forever.

With thoughts of Gracie in his head, he twisted the doorknob and stepped outside to the street. The nights were still cool and crisp and he inhaled deeply of the fresh air. This was an advantage. Although Louisville wasn't a smoggy town, the air seemed cleaner here. He stood for a moment taking in the quiet, then leaned against the bricked front of his building. About the same time, a light went on next door in Gracie's shop, throwing a muted rectangular glow toward the street.

Images of her this morning popped into his brain. That same image had troubled him all day long. He couldn't deny that right from the start, he'd thought Ms. Grace Hart an attractive woman. Geekmeister's had kept him so busy though, that he'd only allowed himself to entertain those thoughts briefly over the past three weeks.

But since seeing her this morning, with her hair soft around her shoulders and wearing nothing more than that big, sexy t-shirt—well, he was having difficulty extracting thoughts of her from his mind.

Beside him, the door handle jiggled and the door swung open to Gracie's shop. Carson stood still, waiting, barely allowing himself to breathe.

She stepped out, a huge watering can in hand, and moved toward the edge of the street, where she started watering two large flower boxes full of pansies. Carson watched her with fascination. He decided right then that he really liked her hair down, not in the French roll she often twisted her locks up into. Tonight, over the T-shirt, she wore a short, wraparound robe of pale blue. Even though the robe covered the T-shirt quite well, it still only hit her a little below mid-thigh, and didn't do a lot to hide those gorgeous legs.

With a long sigh, he let his gaze stretch all the way down to her bare feet and painted toenails. A leg man, he wasn't the least bit disappointed that Gracie had decided to show her legs.

She moved to the other side of the flower boxes, nearly facing him now, and Carson decided not to play voyeur any longer. He stepped away from the building and closer to the flowers.

"Those pesky, thirsty plants. Always need the water, huh?" he said rather loudly. Immediately, he wished he'd taken another tactic.

Startled, Gracie jerked her head up and let out a little shriek. One hand flew to her chest while the other dropped the watering can sharply on her toe.

"Ow!"

"Damn!"

Carson rushed forward.

Gracie stumbled backward and sat on the side of the flower box, her chest still heaving. She pulled the injured foot up and laid it on her right knee, then looked up at Carson. "You scared the hell out of me!"

He sat across from her on the opposite flower box. "God, Gracie, I'm sorry. I didn't mean to—"

She waved him off and reached for her foot. "It's okay. Just dropped the damned thing on my toe."

Carson reached over and righted the metal watering can, then also reached for Gracie's foot. "Let me see."

"It's okay." She shook her head and covered her foot with her hands.

"No. Please."

Reaching out, Carson gently took the sole of her foot in his hands, cradling it in his palm. Her hands slid back. Lifting his gaze to her face, he made eye contact with Gracie as he carefully ran his hand along the top of the arch of her foot.

She grimaced. "Ow!"

"Where does it hurt? Here?" He pushed along the top of her toes.

"The two middle ones."

He probed some more.

She jerked her foot back. "Ouch!"

"There?"

"What do you think?" she bit back.

Carson laughed. "Yeah. I think there."

"Is it broken?" Her voice was softer as she asked, leaning forward as if to inspect the toe.

"Hard to tell," he answered her.

"It hurts."

With her foot still cradled in his palm, Carson began a slow caress of both the bottom and top of her foot. Instinctively, she jerked back, but he held her foot a little tighter, gently resisting the pull. He didn't know why, but he wanted to touch her, to make her feel better. And as he continued the slow massage of her foot and each of its tiny appendages, he resisted the temptation to look up into her face.

The night had suddenly gone still around them. Not a breath; not a breeze. Nothing moved. Except his heart, which was beginning a slow and steady thrum in his chest.

Then suddenly, the night seemed full of just the two of them.

Finally, he looked up at Gracie. "Better?"

Her eyes were big and full of question. The expression on her face was difficult to discern. Quickly, she broke the connection between them and withdrew her foot. Carson dropped his hands to his side.

"Yes." She cleared her throat and stood. "It's . . . it's fine now. Thank you."

"Just a pretty good whack, I guess. I don't think it's broken."

In the next movement, she gathered the watering can and turned toward the door. "Guess we'll see. It's late. I should be getting inside."

Carson nodded. "You sure you're okay?"

"Yes. I'm fine." She started for her door, a slight hobble in her step.

Carson stepped up behind her. "I really am sorry I startled you. I didn't mean to do that."

As they both stood in front of her door, she turned and faced him again. "I know. It's okay. I'm sure it will be fine by morning." Then she offered him one of those little, uncertain grins he liked.

He nodded and she reached for the doorknob.

"Wait."

She looked at him, questioning.

"I . . . uh . . . Friday night I'm giving a little party. Just a few of my friends from Louisville. To kick off the opening of the cafe. I'd like for you to come. That is, if you don't have other plans."

Suddenly, the thought occurred to him that it was quite possible she might have a date. He didn't like the notion of that.

She bit her lip and glanced away.

"Just a small get-together," he added. "Izzie will be there, too."

She looked back at him and continued to chew her lip.

"Even if for a little while?"

Then after another lengthy moment, she dropped her chin in a nod. "I'll be out of town Wednesday through Friday on a buying trip. If I'm not too tired when I get back late Friday afternoon, I'll come by," she finally said.

Then she twisted the doorknob and walked back into her shop. Carson wondered why all of a sudden the night appeared so empty again.

# SEVEN

Murphy's Law must truly exist.

A storm delayed Gracie's flight into Boston on Wednesday until way after midnight, which in turn forced her to take a cab to her hotel, a cab for which she had to pay an exorbitant price. The cabbie was new and didn't know how to get to the hotel, made several wrong turns, and charged her for every one of them. Then, the hotel desk clerk told her she had no knowledge of Gracie's reservation. Luckily, Gracie produced the confirmation number posthaste and they were forced to give her a nice suite for her original price.

It was the only good thing that happened the entire trip.

Thursday, she acquired a touch of food poisoning; she assumed the culprit was the marinated calamari she'd eaten for lunch. The remainder of her evening was spent in the bathroom.

Friday morning, she had a dispute with a vendor at a lingerie show and ended up abruptly canceling the order she'd come specifically to Boston to get.

Angry at herself, she almost missed her flight home, then found out that due to more weather disturbances, her flight was rerouted through Atlanta, where she endured a four-hour layover.

Besides all that, her toe had turned black and was still mighty tender. She was almost certain it was broken.

By the time she was ready to pull into her parking spot behind the shop around ten o'clock Friday evening, Gracie knew the only thing on her agenda for the remainder of the night would be to fall into bed and oblivion for the next ten hours or so.

Except there was one small problem.

There was no empty parking space behind her shop. Not even the space reserved for her, marked "private parking." Carson's red Corvette was parked in his space, however, right next to it.

There were no empty spaces behind either shop.

Or even on the street in front of the shop.

What was going on?

Finally, her anger and her blood pressure rising, she parked three blocks away in the bank parking lot, retrieved her luggage from the trunk of her Miata, then hurriedly wheeled and hobbled her way up the sidewalk, grumbling all the while.

This last hurdle did not put her in a good mood.

For the life of her, she couldn't figure out who would have the audacity to park in her private parking space behind her own home!

She was tired, dammit!

She'd had a helluva past three days.

Her toe hurt.

And she just wanted to go home. To bed! Such a simple thing.

Before the night was through, someone was going to cough up some explanations. The more she thought about it, the angrier she became.

About a block away from her shop, she heard the music. It did nothing to lift her spirits.

Party. Damn. Someone was having a party.

*Party?*

*Friday night?*

*Carson?*

Stopping abruptly, she cocked her head to one side. No, certainly it wasn't Carson. A little get-together with friends, he'd said. Izzie would be there, too.

Something wasn't right.

Slowly, she walked closer to the cafe, and the music grew louder. And louder. Glancing toward the street, she noticed a city police cruiser making a slow progression past the shops. Both hers and Carson's.

She picked up her step. Alternative rock filled her ears.

Finally, she came to a halt directly in front of Carson's cafe. The door was open, music and laughter and some kind of ping-ping-pong-poinging sound poured out to the street. What in the world?

Gracie glanced through the window. People. Everywhere. Wall to wall.

People with drinks.

People playing cards.

People laughing.

People playing some sort of . . . video games?

People watching some sporting event on a gargantuan television screen?

What had happened to quaint and Victorian?

Then she glanced *at* the window. Painted across the large, shopfront window, in huge red-and-green script, were the words Geekmeister's CyberCafe.

Gracie grimaced. What the hell is a cybercafe? Or a geekmeister for that matter?

She didn't want to know.

What she *did* want to know, however, was the reason why Carson Price had lied to her.

He had turned the other half of her building into a bar!

Then she heard her name being shouted from somewhere beyond her vision. She searched the crowd in Carson's "cafe," trying to figure out who would have the audacity to call her into such a place.

"Gracie!"

Carson glanced up sharply from where he was mixing a Bahama Mama when he heard Amie yell out Gracie's name. The moment of truth was upon him. Thank God he'd had the sense to invite Amie. She was a party demon and already in love with the concept of Geekmeisters. He was sure he'd already wooed her to his side.

Watching as Amie made her way through the crowd, drink in hand, Carson knew Gracie wouldn't be as easily convinced. In fact, he'd been dreading this encounter the entire evening. And from the looks of things, Gracie wasn't too keen on what she was seeing.

Gracie gestured and glanced agitatedly from side to side as she spoke to Amie. The body language wasn't positive; that was for sure. Amie, in turn, smiled and excitedly pointed at this and that around the room, as if doing a hard sell on her friend.

"C'mon, Amie," he whispered under his breath. "Convince her." He wasn't sure of the reason he wanted so badly for Amie to convince Gracie that Geekmeister's was an okay thing; he just knew that it mattered. The most likely reason, of course, was that he wanted to stay here. Subconsciously, he thought there might be another reason he wasn't quite as quick to explore.

So he stayed put behind the bar, watching for an adverse reaction from Gracie. She didn't look much past Amie, who was talking fast and furiously now. Then Gracie looked up and her gaze met head-on with his and locked for several seconds.

*Uh-oh.*

The next instant she made a beeline directly toward the bar, suitcase still in tow, dodging party-goers as she made her slow, half-limping progression across the room.

When she reached him, she narrowed her gaze, tilted her chin in an effort of authority, threw back her shoulders, and shouted loudly over the music and laughter. "Mr. Price, may I have a word with you?" She glanced from right to left then and continued, "In private."

*Mr. Price.*

He didn't like the sound of that but decided to just go with it. Nodding, he returned, "Of course. This way."

Carson led the way to the back room and didn't look behind him as Gracie followed. When they reached the storage room-slash-office, he turned to let her pass then closed the door behind the two of them.

The music was muffled; the atmosphere inside the room was still charged. It had nothing to do with the party.

"How was your trip?" He thought he'd try to get things off on a positive note.

"Lousy," she bit back. "I got food poisoning. I had a four-hour layover in Atlanta. I lost a contract. And my toe is black."

That wasn't the note he wanted to start off with.

"I'm sorry to hear—"

"And *then*, Mr. Price, I come home to find out I can't even park in my *own* parking space and that my tenant next door is a liar and has turned my building into a bar. A bar! My God, what kind of lowlife do you expect to drag in here!"

*Tenant. Liar.*

He didn't like the sound of those words, either.

Carson put up his hands. "Whoa. Wait a minute. Let's talk about this."

She frowned and crossed her arms over her chest.

Carson continued. "I have no intention of pulling in degenerates off the street. This is as much of a family thing as it is a bar."

"*Family* thing?" she screeched. Her arms fell to her side and her eyes widened in disbelief of his words.

He was beginning to think this wasn't a good time to talk to her about it.

"Yes, family thing. It's just a glorified arcade, Gracie, with computer games and a wide-screen TV and the option of a drink and a sandwich while you're here. Kids can go off and do their thing while parents relax with a glass of wine or a beer and watch the game. We can have birthday parties and music on the weekends. Family entertainment, Gracie. That's all it is."

"That's certainly *not* what it looks like tonight."

"Well, tonight is just some of my friends and their friends . . ."

"And their friends," she continued, glancing back at the door. Carson had to admit that more people had come than he'd expected.

"I certainly hope," she continued, "that you're not intending to be up making this racket at all hours of the night because I, for one, am extremely tired and would like about ten hours of sleep." She turned toward the door, then whipped around again. "We'll talk about this tomorrow, Mr. Price. I'm not in the right frame of mind to discuss business at the moment. But I want to tell you one thing, I'm not pleased about this. Not one bit."

*Business.*

With that, she left, slamming the door.

Carson stared after her. "Well, that certainly went well," he muttered to himself.

* * *

Gracie told herself that she was simply going to block it all from her head, consume a fistful of ibuprofen, and pray that sleep would not elude her. Tomorrow, when her head was clear and she could think rationally, she'd deal with Mr. Carson Price.

Yes, that's what she would do.

But first, she had to get her ducks all in a row. There was no way she was going to let Carson Price's business next door ruin her business—the business she'd worked so hard to build.

Punching her pillow and wadding it up into a tight little ball, she shoved it under her head, closed her eyes tightly, and tried to erase the scene still etched in her mind from moments earlier.

A bar. No way.

Carson Price was insane.

There had to be some way out of that lease. Tomorrow, she would find it.


"What do you mean there is nothing we can do?" Gracie paced from one corner of Jim Gray's massive oak desk to the other, her head shaking and her arms firmly crossed over her chest. "There has got to be something, some loophole. Look again."

"Nope. Gracie, look, I told you. It's clean as a pin. No loopholes. Everything above board, no tricks, no fine print. Nothing to make the lease null and void. Your signature clinched this deal. I'm sorry, hon, but he's got the place for a year. If you breach the contract, you're gonna owe him a heck of a lot of money."

Stopping, Gracie turned to look at Jim, her father's childhood friend and her attorney. He'd never once steered her wrong before. There was no reason not to believe him now.

"I was so stupid to sign the lease that he drew up."

"Wouldn't have been any different had he signed the one you drew up, Gracie. A signed contract is a signed contract. You willingly put your signature there. He just tightened up a few things and made a couple of others a little broad, all to his advantage, of course, but nothing out of the ordinary."

"So, it's legal."

"Every bit of it."

"But he said he was going to open a cafe."

"And he did."

"But he didn't!"

"Oh, yes, Gracie, he did."

"But not the kind I *thought* he was going to open!"

"That's your perception, honey, not his. He did what he said he was going to do. Even wrote into the lease that he planned to apply for a liquor license."

Gracie threw up her hands. "Well, I assumed he was going to serve wine and cheese or something!"

"Well, he decided to serve *or something,*" Jim replied.

Gracie wanted to scream and shout and stomp her feet on the floor and throw a temper tantrum. She hated being frustrated. And she hated being duped all the more.

Finally, she plopped into the leather armchair across from Jim's desk and slumped into a most unladylike posture. "I give up."

"You could fight it."

She arched a brow and sat up a little straighter. "I could?" Maybe there was hope yet.

Jim nodded. "Yes. But you'd lose. And it would be expensive. I wouldn't advise it."

Her arched brow fell.

"Besides, he's an attorney, and a damned good one to boot. I don't think either one of us wants to cross him."

Gracie slumped back into the chair and frowned. Money was not something she was rolling in, and she really didn't want to make an enemy of Carson. She just didn't want a bar next door. It could ruin everything. "I guess I cooked my own goose, didn't I?"

Jim leaned closer. "Not necessarily. If I know you, Gracie, you'll find some way to make all this work *for* you and not against you."

She glanced away. How in the world would a bar next door work positively for a place like Romantically Yours? She couldn't think of one single advantage.


Carson looked up from his work at the bar and stared out the shop window toward the street. What was that noise?

Listening, he cocked his head to one side.

Silence.

After a minute, he glanced back down at the paperwork spread out before him.

*Crash!*

He glanced back up. Yes. That was something. Definitely something.

*"Izzie?"* He looked to the ceiling, wondering what the child was doing upstairs.

At that point, he heard another crash. Then a shriek. And he knew both noises definitely weren't coming from upstairs.

They were coming from next door.

"Ah, hell," he muttered and quickly rose. "Please don't let that be Izzie."

He rushed out his front door and into Gracie's shop, not having to stop to open her door because it was wide open. The scene that met him made his stomach plummet to the floor.

First and foremost, he'd never seen a cat as large as Gracie's old shop cat, Claire, move as quickly as she was moving at that precise moment. It appeared she was doing three-hundred-and-sixty degree rotations inside the shop, under tables, over chairs, leaping onto display cabinets, sliding over polished hardwood floors, tipping crystal goblets, and knocking over brass candlesticks. All the while she was making hissing noises that he'd never heard come from any earthly cat before.

But that was probably due to the fact that Izzie's nymph of a Shih-Tzu pup was hot on Claire's heels, nipping and yipping, ears flying and toenails clicking, leaping and sliding and knocking things over right behind her.

On her tail was Izzie. A shoeless Izzie who, in the process of chasing both cat and pup, managed to slide with an excited yelp into a table display full of Victorian cards and papers. The table skidded into a mannequin draped in a satin robe. The mannequin teetered, papers flew high into the air and then landed haphazardly around all of them like a game of fifty-two pickup, while Izzie sprawled out spread-eagle on the floor, finally coming to rest beneath the table.

He heard a small *oomph* as she hit the wall. Carson grimaced.

And bringing up the rear, her long skirt flowing, several tendrils of hair escaping from her French roll, her high heels clicking on the floor, was Gracie. Just before she reached his daughter, he heard her cry out as one of her heels caught on the edge of an oriental throw rug, sending her tumbling under the table with Izzie.

A larger *oomph* reached his ears. He grimaced again.

Then the mannequin fell with another loud crash. The entire scenario must have happened in no less than five seconds flat.

Hell, Carson thought. This wasn't good.

This wasn't good at all.

He raced toward the woman and the girl. The cat and the pup were long gone. At this moment, he didn't even care where they were long gone to.

"Are you two all right?"

Reaching under the table, he grasped Gracie's forearm, trying to ignore that her skirt had ridden up to her thigh, and helped her into a sitting position. She thanked him, rubbed an elbow, and then helped him go after Izzie. Together they pulled her from underneath the table until she, too, was sitting before them.

Izzie rubbed the back of her head.

"You guys all right?" Carson repeated.

"Yes," Gracie finally said, only a slight scowl on her face.

Izzie nodded.

Carson watched as Gracie lifted a hand to her hair and attempted to smooth back the wayward strands into her clip as she glanced about the room, covertly surveying the damages.

"Don't look," he told her.

Heaving a big sigh and then exhaling in a short huff, she looked back to Carson. "And why shouldn't I look?"

"Because it will only depress you."

"But I have to—"

"In a minute."

She stared at him. "In a minute, what?"

"In a minute you can assess the damages and add up the bill and start cleaning up. And I'll help you." He looked down at his daughter now, who had remained extremely quiet the past few minutes. "And so will Izzie. We'll gladly pay for the damages."

Izzie frowned and looked to the floor.

Carson let it go for now. He looked back to Gracie.

"I have a good idea what happened. I hope that this—"

Gracie waved him off and stood. Carson stood with her. "Mr. Price, it's not her fault. Really. I let Izzie bring the pup in. I didn't think Claire would react like that. It's not the child's fault. It's mine."

"But—"

Gracie smoothed her skirt and straightened her sweater. Tilting her head back, she looked him square in the eyes. "Don't blame her. Please, just go find your pup. I think both animals ran out the back door. Don't worry about Claire. She'll find her way home."

Carson glanced down at Izzie then; her eyes were wide.

"Bandit went out the back door?"

Gracie crouched down to speak to her. "I'm not sure. Why don't you go look?"

Izzie glanced to her father and he nodded his permission. The child shouted for her pup. After she was gone, Carson looked back to Gracie. Hell, he didn't need this today. She was mad enough at him already. One more incident like this and she might actually have grounds to boot them out.

"You don't have to take up for her if she did something wrong, you know," he told her. "I want her to learn to own up to her mistakes."

Gracie just stared at him. "Mr. Price, she's a beautiful child. A mischievous child, yes. But this one was not her fault. I'm not blaming you. Or her. It was me. So go help your daughter find your pup and quit worrying."

It was blunt, but Carson wasn't really surprised. She'd been blunt the past couple of days. Still, he'd expected that she'd want them to take the blame. He'd been wrong.

Carson stood for a moment longer looking at Miss Grace Hart. For the life of him, he couldn't figure the woman out. First she ran hot, then cold. First she's mad, then she's not.

Kept him damned confused.

Too damned confused.

That's what worried him.

*Women.*

# EIGHT

"Are you mad at my dad?"

Gracie stopped counting the money in her cash drawer and peered across the counter at Izzie. There she stood, the epitome of tomboy, scuffed knees peeking out from beneath cut-off denims, lopsided ponytail sticking out from a crookedly placed ball cap, dirt-smudged cheeks, and floppy high-tops with the laces untied. On her left hand was a ball glove; in her right, a softball.

Taking a moment to assess the child, Gracie had to smile. When she was Izzie's age, she'd been exactly the opposite of this child. Nothing but frilly dresses, ribbons and bows, and dancing shoes. No ball gloves for her.

Still, she was captivated by Izzie. Even though she didn't want to admit it, she adored the child.

It was late Thursday afternoon and June had turned hot and humid, but it was relatively cool in the shop, even though the air conditioner was forced to run solidly. Izzie insisted on skipping in and out of the shop all afternoon and Gracie had made only one rule about that—no Bandit was to skip in and out with her. She'd finally recovered from the incident earlier in the week.

But she was certain the fanning front door was causing another problem, elevating the shop's temperature several degrees.

Gracie wiped a trickle of perspiration from her temple.

She liked the child. Had grown quite fond of her over the last two weeks. Izzie had made her presence quite well known in and out of the shop. And surprisingly, Gracie didn't mind. Not one bit. Not even after what had happened with the animals.

She wasn't mad at the child at all.

She *was* still upset with the father.

"Or are you mad at me?"

Surprised, Gracie glanced down at the imp. "No, honey," she replied. "I'm not mad at you! And I'm really not mad at your father, either," she told Izzie. "It's just that we're having a bit of a . . . misunderstanding. That's all."

Izzie cocked her head to one side and stared at Gracie. "Yeah, right."

The child always threw her a curve ball.

"You don't believe me?"

Izzie shook her head. "Nope."

"And why not?" Gracie finished counting the bills, banded them, and slid them into her money pouch with the checks. Now she was going after the change.

Izzie leaned her elbows on the counter. Her little chin practically rested on the smooth oak surface; she was barely tall enough to see over the thing.

"Well," she began, "my dad has been grumpy all week and you didn't stay long at the party last Friday and he yells and tells me to stay away and not bother you and he still says we're going to pay for the broken stuff and you won't talk to him. I saw you ignoring him when you were watering the flowers last night. And he won't talk to you. I saw him ignoring you at Amie's Place the other morning at breakfast. And—"

Gracie put up a hand. "Stop. I get the picture, Izzie. Perceptive little girl, aren't you?"

She grinned from ear to ear and nodded. "What does *per-cep-a-tive* mean?"

Gracie smiled back at the scamp. "It means that you notice things."

The child nodded furiously this time. "I notice lots of things."

"Oh, you do?"

"Yep."

"Is that why you think your father and I are mad at each other?"

Izzie pretended to think about that a minute. She cocked her head to one side, laid a forefinger beside her chin, and chewed on her lip. After a moment, she snapped her finger and said, "I got it! I know why you're mad at each other!"

Gracie cleared her throat. "Now, Izzie. I told you. I'm not mad at your father. It's just a misunderstanding between the two of us and—"

"It has something to do with the eye thing, doesn't it?"

Now Gracie was puzzled. "The eye thing?"

"Uh-huh. The eye thing."

"I don't think I understand."

Izzie thought another moment. "Well . . . it's something my dad does when—"

The bell over the front door tinkled and both Gracie and Izzie turned toward the sound. In strode Carson. Every long-legged, spit-shined and polished inch of him. Gracie gulped. Definitely a nice-looking specimen of male anatomy, she told herself. She guessed he was getting ready to open for so-called "dinner" at five.

Too bad that she was angry with the man. Funny how she had to keep reminding herself.

She couldn't help but notice that Geekmeister's CyberCafe had sported a small crowd every evening this week thus far. Not that she wished the man bad luck in his business; she was just hoping that if business were bad, it might solve her dilemma.

And she could use an easy solution to a dilemma for once in her lifetime.

In a couple of steps, Carson was beside his daughter. "Izzie, I told you not to bother Ms. Hart."

Grace noticed he didn't look her in the eyes. She didn't even flinch at the reference to *Ms. Hart.* That was the way it had been all week. Their conversations were stiff and to the point, with little elaboration. Carson appeared sorely uncomfortable around her and she . . . well, she just flat out wasn't sure she could trust him. So, she'd decided to stay out of his way and entertain little conversation from the man until she decided what could be done about the entire situation.

Which, according to Jim, would probably be very little.

"She's not a bother, *Mr. Price*. Really, she's not."

"Well, she shouldn't be here. I asked her not to keep running in and out of your shop all day long. Especially after the other day . . ."

He didn't finish the sentence. Gracie shook her head. "It's not a problem. Slow day. Actually, she's been a lot of company."

He grasped Izzie's hand and started for the door. Briefly, he made eye contact with Gracie. "Well, it's time for her to go. C'mon, Iz."

"But, Dad," the child interrupted, "I was just starting to tell Gracie about—"

"Oh, that's right," Gracie interrupted. "There was something she was going to tell me. Could you wait just a minute?" Gracie suddenly got the distinct impression that Carson was in a terrible hurry to get away.

Did she dare toss a kink in his impatience?

He exhaled deeply, glanced from woman to child, and said restlessly, "All right. What is it?"

"The eye thing, Dad. I was going to tell her about the eye thing."

Gracie watched as Carson flushed from his neck to the top of his head in about one-quarter of a second flat. Suddenly, it was quite obvious that Carson didn't want to talk about the eye thing.

"Yes, she was just about to tell me about the eye thing," Gracie goaded. "Curious thing, the eye thing. Such a mystery, I understand." Gracie didn't know why, but she sort of felt like putting Carson Price on the spot.

Much the way she had felt put on the spot the other night.

She tried to smother a giggle.

Carson threw back his shoulders, grasped Izzie's hand a little tighter, and took one backward step toward the door. He glared at his child then turned to Gracie.

"That silly eye thing?" he laughed. "What a joker she is. It's a little trick she uses sometime. She'll have to show you when there's more time. Something she learned from her grandpa. Right now, we have to be somewhere and—"

"But, Dad, that's not—"

"We have to go now, Iz." His words grew sterner. He turned to Gracie. "Sorry to bother you, Ms. Hart. We'll . . . um . . . talk to you later."

"See! There, Dad. That's it! See, Gracie? He's doing it—"

Gracie immediately looked at Carson. His eyes had closed about halfway, one brow was arched, and a little come-hither twinkle flashed from beneath that arched brow.

Ahhhh . . . that kind of eye thing, Gracie realized. Wanting desperately to giggle, she didn't, deciding instead just to glance away.

Instantly, he whisked the child out of the shop before Gracie's brain really had a chance to grasp the entire truth about the eye thing. No matter, she thought. By the look on Izzie's face, and the little wink she'd tossed her as she left, she was sure to spill it sooner or later.

Besides, Gracie had a pretty good idea just exactly what the eye thing was all about. A girl just knew things like that.

The latest, hottest romance novel was up for discussion at the Book Club on Friday night. Constance was tired of discussing bestsellers, she'd told the group the month before. Gracie was sure her friend was up to something that didn't have anything at all to do with books, but more with romance. She wished she'd give it a break.

The once-a-month Friday night group was different from the weekly Saturday morning group, with the exception of Constance. She was pretty much a staple item around Romantically Yours. Gracie had never minded, of course, until lately. All Constance seemed to want to talk about was Geekmeister's and the geek next door who owned the joint and how he might fit in with Gracie's romantic whims.

Or the lack of such a thing.

The thing was, Gracie knew her life was missing something. She *knew* she'd be happier with a man in her life. With a child in her life. With a family. That's what that ticking clock thing was all about. But it was difficult for her to put herself out there, and she really and truly didn't want Constance and Amie butting into her love life any longer.

She just didn't have the heart to tell them.

She was glad, however, for one thing. It seemed

Geek's had become the newest interest in their lives of late. Thank goodness. Perhaps they'd let her be for a while. Even though it stung a little bit.

Like Amie, Constance was becoming a Geek's groupy. Were all her friends insane? They used to be *her* groupies!

Constance glanced at her watch. "I wish Bets would get here," she said for the third time. "I'd like to get this discussion started and on its way."

Three other ladies nodded in agreement, Gracie not included. In no hurry, she sat back and watched Ellen Harper, the Methodist church pianist, Wanda Martin, the high school home economics teacher, and Kelly Brooks, who just graduated from cosmetology school, glance from one to the other and then back to flip through the book-marked pages of their books.

Something was amiss. She wasn't quite sure what.

Gracie glanced at her watch. "You ladies gonna turn into pumpkins or something at the stroke of seven?" she asked.

Kelly glanced up. "Happy hour ends at eight," she stated, then returned to her book.

Gracie dipped her head in a slow nod. Hmmmm . . .

"Drinks are half price until then," Wanda added. Ahhh-haaa!

"Thought we'd finish early and take in a little Friday night activity at Geek's," Constance concluded. "Of course, with Bets' being late, we might have to make it another time."

Gracie smiled. They *were* her groupies after all!

The Book Club was important to them, she knew, and they wouldn't give it up for something as silly as—

"Happy hour only comes once a week, you know, so we wouldn't want to miss it," Ellen Harper chimed in.

Gracie widened her eyes and took in the expression on the woman's face. This same woman, who had to be pushing sixty, who had taught her piano lessons when she was a child and who had drilled Bible verses into her head in Sunday school for years, was a Geek's groupie, too?

"Ellen?" Gracie was aghast.

Ellen cocked her head and stared back. "Gracie! Don't look at me like that! I'm a grown woman and can do whatever I wish."

Shaking herself, Gracie nodded in agreement. "Well, yes . . . I didn't mean anything. I just didn't think you—"

Outside the shop door, a woman's shriek interrupted her comment. All eyes turned toward the sound. Through the glass of the shop window, Gracie could see Betsy Baker, the twice-widowed town librarian, standing very still, her arms shoved out from her body as if in surprise, her eyes wide, her face turned skyward.

She appeared to be dripping. Water-soaked. To the skin. Hair and clothing to boot.

*Oh my.*

Simultaneously, Gracie and the others jumped up and raced toward Bets only to hear a *splunsh!* as the door opened. Bets wailed again and looked upward.

Gracie, reaching the scene first, glanced up only to see the tip of a ponytail fly back into the window of Carson's apartment.

*What in the world?*

Gracie looked back at Bets—mouth still agape, dripping huge droplets of water from the tip of her nose, hair plastered against her skull—and then to the concrete sidewalk.

Balloon bits.

Water balloon bits.

Everywhere.

"Bets! Come in here! Quickly!" Gracie ushered her friend inside and through the shop, where she planted her in a chair in her office. "I'll run upstairs and get some towels."

*That child! What had gotten into her?*

*No time to ponder that now,* she thought.

Quickly, she snatched some towels from her linen closet and headed back down the stairs. She was almost certain she caught sight of Izzie peeking out through a crack in Carson's door. Later. For now she had to take care of Bets.

"Here we go," she said breathlessly as she entered her office again.

Bets looked up at her, hair still stringing down her face. "Now what am I going to do? I had my hair all fixed and everything!" she whined.

Gracie knelt beside her and started daubing a towel around her face. "I'm so sorry, Bets. I'm sure your hair was beautiful. For the life of me I can't imagine . . ."

But that was a lie. She could easily imagine. She
st didn't know why.

Bets' shoulders dropped. "I just had it done this
ternoon," she whined some more. "It was a new
t, new style. It was the new me. I couldn't wait to
ow it to all of you."

The women all consoled her. Constance rubbed
r back; Kelly murmured comforting words. Ellen
tted her hand.

"And I was so looking forward to Happy Hour."

Gracie stood, not believing what she was hearing.
ad they *all* gone mad?

"Happy Hour?"

All five women looked up and nodded. Gracie
ought they were a pitiful sight.

"What in the world is this sudden captivation
th Happy Hour?" she asked. "What about the
ok Club? What about our discussion of the hot-
st, sexiest romance novel to come down the pike
quite some time?" She picked the book up off
r desk and turned to Constance. "Huh? What
out this? You couldn't wait to discuss this last
onth, and now the lot of you can't wait to get
t of here and go get happy with some geeks next
or!"

All five women just stared at her, the blankest
oks on their faces Gracie thought she'd ever seen.

"You just don't understand, do you, Gracie?"

"That's right, I don't. We've been doing the Friday
ight Book Club for years. Now that this . . . this
eekmeister's thing is next door, you have all but
rgotten about the Book Club and me."

Constance cleared her throat and stepped forward. "That's not true, Gracie. We had every intention of bringing you with us."

That statement, which was certainly intended to make Gracie feel better, didn't.

"But I don't *want* to go to Geekmeister's!"

The women sat stunned before her. Gracie hadn't meant to shout, but she had. It took several seconds, then Bets stood and turned to Kelly. "You think you could fix this hair of mine?"

It was as if Gracie had been totally and absurdly dismissed.

Kelly nodded furiously and smiled. "Let me try."

"All right." She turned to Grace. "Got a blow dryer around here?"

Dumbfounded, Gracie nodded and pointed toward the bathroom. Kelly retrieved the thing and, in a matter of minutes, had coifed and dried and fluffed to Bets' satisfaction.

"There," she proclaimed.

Bets looked in the mirror from all angles.

"I love it," declared Constance.

"Gorgeous," exclaimed Ellen.

"You're a whiz with a blow-dryer, girl," Wanda added.

"Not too shabby," Kelly remarked, surveying her work from several angles.

"You really like it?" asked Bets.

"Uh-huh," the other women chimed in unison.

"Then let's go."

"Wait! Blow-dry my shirt!" she told Kelly.

Bets had no longer flung the words from her

outh than Kelly had dried her clothes as well and
ch of them scrambled for the door. To Gracie, it
as like something out of some insane Lucy-and-
hel spoof.

They'd all gone mad. She was convinced.

Before she realized it, Gracie put two fingers be-
een her lips and whistled the most unladylike
histle she'd whistled in her life. She owed that to
er cousin Eric, who'd taught her how to do that
hen she was twelve.

The crew stopped dead in their tracks and slowly
rned to look at her. Kelly still had her blow dryer
her hand.

"Just where in the hell do the five of you think
u are going?"

Constance squared her shoulders and looked Gra-
e straight in the eyes. "To Geek's," she challenged.

Gracie gulped and stared Constance right back.

She was losing her groupies.

She didn't quite know what to do about it.

"Well?" Constance prompted.

Gracie glanced from one woman to another, took
deep breath, squared her shoulders just like Con-
ance, and drew herself up into her full five-foot-
n-inches height. It was now or never.

"Without me?" she squeaked.

A small grin curled at one corner of Constance's
outh and snaked around to the other side, pro-
ucing a full grin. Gracie hated herself at that pre-
se second in time.

Constance had won.

Damn.

\* \* \*

Carson glanced up just as the entourage entered Geek's. His gaze trailed the crew as the older woman named Constance, followed by her Friday night cohorts, picked their way through the sparse crowd toward the bar. He had to stifle a smile. Two Friday nights in a row. Wonder what Gracie would think.

But just as those words turned over in his brain, Gracie stepped right through his door behind them, startling him.

"Damn," he whispered. "What does she want?" He found it odd that, since she'd chosen to avoid him most of the week, she would venture in for Happy Hour.

There had to be a reason.

Probably wanted to blast him because the music was too loud or that his "undesirable" crowd was causing too much "undesirable" traffic in front of her shop or that he was stealing her customers or something, he thought.

But he was completely taken by surprise when she didn't even toss a glance his way and simply made a beeline straight toward Constance and her cronies. She looked neither right nor left but kept her gaze on her friends. He was even more puzzled when she sidled up to the bar and slipped her delicate little behind onto a bar stool, her back stiff and her heels daintily hooked on a stretcher beneath the stool.

She looked about as comfortable as a gobbler on hanksgiving eve.

He'd waited all week for some indication that she anted him to leave. Particularly after the Bandit ning. He'd spoken briefly and succinctly to her a w times later in the week. A quick "good morn- g" in the stairwell or a cordial "hello" at Amie's. e'd sensed she was edgy, contemplating and choos- g her words carefully, as though she had a whole t she wanted to say to him but was waiting for the recise moment or exactly the right words to enter er head before she commenced.

It was driving him crazy. He needed to know what er intentions were about his lease.

Of course, the lease was airtight. He knew that for ertain. He didn't want to, nor would he, push the sue—but he had an airtight case for keeping the ase at least a year.

He couldn't go back to Louisville now. He'd ulled Izzie out of school, turned over his law prac- ce to Jack, and put his house on the market. There as no turning back. And Gracie Hart didn't know , but she would have a fight on her hands if she nose to back out of their agreement.

Much as he hated to lock horns with her—he ac- ually liked Grace Hart—he would do it, because nat would be the one obstacle in his path to achiev- g his goal.

His goal of a new and stable life for Izzie.

Gracie Hart would not interfere.

No way. No how.

"Barkeep! How 'bout some service over here?"

Carson groaned at Constance's words. He like
the older woman and she was teasing him, h
knew. She was a free-spirited senior citizen wh
spoke her mind and didn't act her age. She alway
made him smile. They'd talked at length a fe
nights earlier about some of her Peace Corps e
periences in the sixties and the years she'd spen
working in the Carter administration in Washing
ton. Interesting woman, to say the least. His groa
had nothing to do with Constance and the fact tha
he was about to take an order for a round o
drinks from her and her friends—friends who n
doubt would hang around awhile tonight—but ha
everything to do with the fact that he would soo
have to face Gracie Hart for more than a brie
encounter.

He might actually have to be pleasant to her.

Ah. Carson had to stifle a small grin. That jus
might be the ticket. Perhaps he should just use hi
manly charms to woo her into compliance.

Truth be known, Gracie's avoidance had bothere
him more than he cared to admit. There were mo
ments when he recalled the scene in front of thei
shops several days back, right after he'd frightene
her and made her drop the watering can on he
toe, that sent a warm surging into his stomach. Th
very instant he'd reached out for her dainty foo
and had attempted to slowly massage away her pai
kept creeping back into his head. He'd felt a sor
of connection that night, something . . .

Wooing Gracie Hart into compliance would no
be a painful task, to say the least.

At that thought, Carson groaned and shook his head. "Last thing you need, Price, is to romance and sweet-talk the woman," he murmured to himself. "You've got enough on your hands without sending out the wrong signals to some unsuspecting female."

Truth was that Carson had no intention of ever getting involved with another woman. Not after experiencing what he had when Marci left. Nope. Never again.

Raising Izzie was his top priority. His *only* priority. Romancing women was . . . well, way on the back burner.

"Woo-hoo . . . Mr. Bartender?" Kelly the cosmetologist waved his way.

Carson glanced back once more to the women and smiled as Kelly grinned widely back and simultaneously winked. Gulping, he plastered a smile on his face and approached them.

"We're ba-ack," one of them chimed.

"I see." Carson smiled. "My Friday night groupies, eh?"

"He's such a cute thing, isn't he?" Ellen patted his hand.

"Come, Carson, be our boy-toy. Won't you?" teased Constance.

Carson felt himself flush.

"Such a love machine. Grrrr . . ." Bets winked lucily and did a little disco move.

"Hubba hubba." That was from Wanda.

Carson caught a glimpse of Gracie as her eyes widened in what looked to be disbelief at the sexual

banter her friends were dishing out. That's whe
Carson decided to get in on the game. Grace Ha
was definitely uncomfortable.

And uncomfortable was definitely cute on her.

He didn't like where his thoughts were leadin
him.

"So what shall we have tonight, ladies? A dip int
a Fuzzy Navel? A Screaming Orgasm? A little Se
on-the-Beach? Or something wilder?"

"Oh! Sex-on-the-Beach! That's what I want!" Elle
called out excitedly. "I haven't had sex on the beac
since Henry died!"

Carson grinned, trying hard not to think abou
Ellen having sex anywhere.

"Ellen, he wants your drink order! Not the detai
of your sex life!" This was from Wanda.

"Oh, but Ellen . . . do tell! Do tell! I wann
know," Kelly insisted.

"Well," she began, "it was 1976, and we were va
cationing in this little place called—"

Abruptly, Gracie stood and blurted out, "My Goc
I can't believe I'm hearing this!"

For the next ten seconds or so, the entire grou
was quiet, all eyes on the tall blonde.

Carson let his gaze shift from Gracie to the fiv
women and back again.

"Gracie, sit down and quit being a prude."

That was from Constance.

Carson watched Gracie's eyes widen even mor
her mouth open, then close, then open and clos
again very quickly. Not even a whimper escaped he
lips.

Then she sat right back down again.
He took drink orders from each of them.
Including Gracie.

# NINE

*There, take that! Let them even think about calling me a prude again.*

With near precision aim, or as much precision aim as she could muster under the circumstances, Gracie sank another olive into the martini glass on the sink. From her seat at the bar, the glass was sitting approximately five feet away on the counter against the wall. With the olive carefully positioned between her thumb and forefinger, she slightly closed one eye and tossed another across the empty space between.

*Plop!*

Oh yes, she was good. The glass was half full already.

And it was only her . . . hmmm . . . what? Her third martini?

Or was it her fourth?

Couldn't tell from the olives piling up in the martini glass, she knew. She'd stolen most of them from behind the bar when Carson wasn't looking.

Oh, hell, she thought. Eating olives and slurping martinis—she'd puff up like a blowfish by morning.

Slowly, Gracie leaned lower into the bar and placed her cheek against the cool, wooden surface. It was late and she was tired. She was also hot. Her brain felt slightly shrink-wrapped. The music from that stupid jukebox was bouncing around inside her skull, not to mention the poinging of those arcade machines. Her eyelids felt as if sandpaper were stuck to the backs of them.

She was most likely a bit tipsy.

But she wasn't a prude.

Nope.

Not Grace Elizabeth Hart.

She was the life of the damned party. Poo poo on Constance and whoever else doubted her party-hardyness. Now, if she just knew where Constance and the others had gone . . .

Perhaps she should take a nap. Just a little one.

"Gracie, wake up, honey. We're leaving."

Gracie sat up like a shot and tried to focus on the face belonging to the voice in front of her, but all she could distinguish was a fuzzy blob of colors that must represent a human being of some sort and a dull pain that landed with a thud across her forehead.

"Huh?"

"Time to go, Sweety."

"Don't wanna." Gracie slunk back down and put her cheek against the bar again. Ahhh . . . that felt so good.

Someone tugged at her arm. "Now, honey. Before you pass out totally and we have to carry you."

Gracie didn't look up, partially waved a leaden

arm at the voice, and closed her eyes. There were more voices behind her, beyond her consciousness almost, but she really didn't care what the voices said.

All she wanted was to sleep . . .

Sometime later she realized the music and the poinging had stopped thrumming in her head and the lights weren't nearly so harsh against her closed eyes and that the wooden counter against her cheek had been replaced with something warm and firm, but yet much softer than the bar.

That was about the same time she realized that someone was quietly talking into her ear—although she couldn't quite understand what that someone was saying—and even through the fuzz and haze of her brain it felt suspiciously like someone had lifted her and was carrying her somewhere . . .

She wasn't quite sure where.

Oh well, it didn't matter, did it?

"Okay, Sleeping Beauty, let's get this over with."

Carson whispered the words ever so softly because he had no desire to wake Gracie from her more-than-tipsy state as he carried her through his bar, ascended the back stairway, stepped through her apartment, and gently deposited her on her antique four-poster bed.

Constance had made sure Gracie's apartment was unlocked before she'd left when it became obvious that the women were not going to budge her from the small nest she'd made at the bar. Luckily, it had been a slow night and Gracie hadn't made a nuisance of herself while she chugged martinis and slam-dunked olives into glasses. She was a quiet drunk, lost in her own little world. Her friends were pretty much amazed, he knew; and when he realized that they were just letting her get drunk, he even questioned why they would do that.

"Do her some good," Constance had said.

"She needs to loosen up a bit," Kelly chimed in.

"She'll be old before her time if she doesn't get out and live a little," Ellen added.

"Been doing nothing but running that shop for ten years," Wanda said. "Shame for a young woman like that to waste away."

"She needs a life," Bets told him.

"She needs a man," Constance said matter-of-factly.

And when those same women just abandoned her, just left her there for him to take care of, he was at first flabbergasted, then furious, then nervous, and then finally extremely curious about the entire situation.

Of course, then it dawned on him.

The old biddies were matchmaking, pure and simple.

They wanted *him* to be Gracie's man.

It was a good thing he had his head screwed on good and tight and he could see through their ploy. He just hoped Gracie did. He sure as hell would hate for her to slip into their matchmaking scheme and fall in love with him, only for him to break her heart.

Because no matter what the Happy Hour Honeys were thinking, Carson Price was *not* the man for Gracie Hart.

Trying to dismiss all that from his head, Carson glanced down at Gracie snuggling into her pillow. She'd curled slightly onto her side after he'd laid her there, drawing her knees up and tucking her hands up next to her chin. Strands of her silky hair had partially fallen from the clip which held it in its usually neat French roll at the back of her head. The clip looked askew and uncomfortable, forcing her head into a crooked position on the pillow.

Contemplating for a second, Carson placed one knee on the bed and reached for the clip. Carefully, he removed it, trying not to tangle and pull her hair. The remainder of her silky mane tumbled about her shoulders. For a second or two, he just stood over her, watching the light from her bedside table lamp dance over the shining highlights of her hair. She moaned and rolled over and Carson moved back. As she twisted to the other side, Gracie's hair fell completely over her face.

Without thinking, he leaned forward again and brushed the locks away from her face, smoothing them back over the pillow. Her hair was soft and so was her cheek where his knuckles briefly touched her.

That was where he made his mistake. And he knew it immediately. That slight touch, that ever-so-gentle caress of his knuckles against her dewy skin and the feel of her silky tresses on the pads of his fingers sent one mega-warning spiral into his gut.

A deep spiral that jackknifed and plummeted into somewhere he'd never felt before.

He had to get out of here.

Abruptly, he pulled back, placed the clip on the bedside table, and reached for the switch on the lamp. But something stopped him and he glanced back once more.

*Oh hell . . .*

With a few jerky and swift movements, he moved to her feet and removed her sandals, careful not to linger over the feel of her foot in his hands, the delicate curve of her arch, or the blaze-red toenails which always took him a bit by surprise. Then he covered her with an afghan lying at the foot of her bed.

There. At least she looked a bit more comfortable.

For the second time, he reached for the lamp, his hand slowing as he glanced at the pictures on her bedside table he hadn't really noticed earlier. Two antique, Victorian-style frames were placed on either side of the lamp. Not sure why, he bent closer to look into one, and then the other.

The first picture was of a woman, a ballet dancer, her hair swept off her face and on top of her head in a tight knot. Her legs were long, her body graceful, her chin tilted high into the air striking an almost regal pose, her arms perfectly placed as she stood in some dancer's position of which he had no clue of the name.

The ballerina, he was certain, was Gracie. A younger Gracie.

That would probably explain the satin ballet slippers placed strategically before the picture.

The other picture was of Gracie and a man . . . which, despite the statements he'd heard earlier this evening, required no explanation at all.

The look between them told all he needed to know. The two were obviously very much in love.


Saturday morning breakfast consisted of a pot of strong coffee, three ibuprofen, and a diuretic. The first to unshrink-wrap her brain, the second to dull the thumping inside her skull, and the third to ward off the puffy blowfish look she woke with from ingesting way too much sodium and alcohol the night before.

It was not a good day.

She was not in the mood for the Saturday morning coffee klatch.

And she wanted like hell to keep the "closed" sign turned out on the door all day long.

But she wouldn't. There had not been a day in ten years, since she first opened the shop, that she'd closed the shop for no reason at all. And the girls were expecting her.

Of course, today could always be a first.

Acting strictly on impulse, Gracie slowly walked to the back of the store and shut off the lights. She ignored the knock on the front door as she slowly made her way back up the stairs.

Gracie Hart certainly wasn't a prude. She'd proven that last night. And she could certainly make her own decisions about whether she wanted to see her friends this morning, or not. Or open her shop this morning, or not.

Today, she chose *or not.*

"All right, so these are our choices. What's it going to be, Munchkin?"

Carson glanced over the shelves at the video store searching for movies suitable for Izzie's eyes and ears. Always careful about his movie selections, he knew the task before him was a difficult one. Izzie was not easily pleased when it came to movies.

What he liked, she didn't. What she liked, or thought she liked, he would never allow.

"Still the same rules?" He glanced back down into her face.

"Yep," she replied. Hands on hips, she cocked her head to one side and ticked them off. "No girlie stuff. No singing movies. No kissie junk. No dopey animals."

Carson grinned. Those rules eliminated quite a bit. His rules were a little different, however. His main concerns were no sex, no foul language, and no violence.

It was damned hard for them to find a happy medium at times. Surely they could agree on something, though.

"All right, so how about *101 Dalmatians* or *Bambi?*"

Izzie snarled her nose and shook her head. "Dopey animals," she replied.

"Okay, well how about this one? *Mary Poppins.*"

She shook her head. "Seen it a hundred times, Dad. Besides, it's a singing movie."

He picked up another. "Here's one." He showed her the box.

"Girlie stuff," she replied.

"This?"

She shook her head. "Kissie junk."

Frustrated, Carson put the box back on the shelf. "Well, there is nothing else, Iz."

"Yes, there is." She raced about three feet to their left and grabbed a movie off the shelf. "What about *Hockey Players from Hell?*"

Carson snatched the box from her hand and studied the picture. A snarling hockey player with blood dripping from his stick stared back at him. What in the world?

"No!"

"But—"

"Too much violence."

"But I watched it at Joey Brockman's house and—"

"You what?" Dumbfounded, Carson looked at his daughter. Wait until he saw Joey Brockman's dad. "Well, you're not going to watch it with me. Let's look over here." He shoved the box back onto the shelf and with a nudge steered her in another direction. The nerve of some parents.

Thank God he'd gotten her out of the city.

"How about this one?" The cover looked safe

enough. He glanced over the blurb on the back. A Cinderella story of the future, it said. He showed it to Izzie.

"Looks like lovey-dovey stuff." She scrunched her nose again.

"I think it looks interesting." Cinderella had to be safe, right?

"No, Dad. I don't wanna—"

"It says it's a kind of Cinderella story. You like Cinderella, don't you?"

Izzie made a rude noise.

Carson tucked it under his arm. "We're getting this one."

"But, Dad . . ." Izzie whined.

"No. This is it. Come on." He began walking toward the counter.

"Ummm . . . you might want to think about that," he heard a female voice behind him say. A very familiar female voice.

Turning, he heard Izzie call out her name before he realized fully who it was behind him.

"Gracie!"

His daughter practically leaped into the woman's arms. "Izzie! Don't jump on Ms. Hart like that!" He pulled on his daughter's arm and gathered her next to his side.

Gracie Hart looked both startled and befuddled, if not a little fatigued. In fact, upon closer inspection, he wasn't quite sure he would have recognized her if Izzie hadn't called out her name.

For the first time since he'd known her, she wasn't wearing a long skirt and sweater or blouse. She was wearing jeans and tennis shoes and a T-shirt. Her hair was pulled through a baseball cap which in turn was pulled down low over her forehead. Underneath the bill of that cap, he could tell her eyes were red-rimmed and swollen.

"Shop closed today?" he queried. He knew Saturday was usually her biggest day of the week. He'd noticed that over the past few weeks.

She nodded slowly. "Feeling a bit under the weather," she told him.

Carson tried like hell not to grin. "Oh."

She glanced away. He decided embarrassed looked cute on her.

"Hope you're feeling better soon."

She nodded again. "I should."

There was another hesitant pause and he said, "Well, we should be on our way." He grasped Izzie's hand and started to turn.

"Wait."

He stopped and looked at Gracie.

Reaching out, she grasped the movie in his hand. "I think you might want to rethink this." She pointed to the rating at the bottom of the movie, which clearly said the movie was rated R. "I don't think you want this one."

Carson studied the back blurb again. Ahhhh . . .

Embarrassed himself now, he looked back at Gracie. "Thanks."

"You're welcome."

"Anytime."

He placed the movie back on the shelf.

"Now we gotta look again?" This was from Izzie.

Exhausted from their movie search, Carson shook his head. "No, I think we'll just go home."

"But, Dad! You promised me a movie!"

He crouched down to look Izzie in the eyes. "I know I did, but there doesn't seem to be anything here that we agree on. So let's just go home and find something else to do. You could try out that new arcade game."

"I don't want to do that!" she wailed. "I'm tired of arcade games. I wanted to watch a movie. You *promised!* You said we'd do something together this Saturday. You said this was our day. You said—"

"Izzie. All right. All right. I did and we will see a movie. How about we go out and see one instead of renting one." He glanced up at Gracie, still embarrassed. He didn't know why Izzie was acting like this.

Gracie looked a mite uncomfortable.

"Well, I guess I'll be seeing you," she said, and waved her hand to Izzie as she started to leave.

"Yes! Dad, I want to go to a movie. Can I invite someone?"

Carson watched Gracie walk away. He hated to admit that he liked the way she looked in those jeans. Not that he didn't like the way she looked in a skirt and silk blouse either, but she just looked very nice in the jeans.

"Dad?"

"What?"

"Can I invite someone to go with us to the movies?"

"*May* I."

"I may?"

He shook his head. "Sure. Of course."

"Great!"

"As soon as we get home you can—"

But she was off in a flash, running down the aisle toward Gracie. He watched her animated display, her excited little jig, and her arms bouncing about as she spoke. He also took in the surprised look on Gracie's face as she glanced back at him and then to Izzie.

She broke away then and started running back toward Carson, a huge grin on her face.

And then it dawned on him.

*Oh, no!*

"It's okay," Izzie told him out of breath. "She said she'd come."


Why in the world she'd agreed to this, she'd never know.

Well, she did know. She'd done it for Izzie. It had a lot to do with how excited the child had seemed, wanting her to join them for the movies. It had everything to do with the sparkle in her eyes and the laughter in her voice. It most certainly had something to do with the way the child pulled at Gracie's heartstrings every time she batted those sinfully long lashes lately.

She adored the child and she wanted to spend more time with her.

*Tick. Tick. Tick.*

It was simple. Gracie Hart was a sucker for the reckless charms of Isabella Price.

That's why she'd told her she'd go to the movies with them. Thing was, she really hadn't thought about the consequences of that decision until just a few moments ago.

"Popcorn?"

Gracie shook her head, feeling extremely awkward. It was almost as if this were a date, and she didn't want it to be a date. In fact, she hadn't been out on a date in, oh . . . say three years or more—and that was with some guy Amie had fixed her up with. Was that the shoe salesman or the jockey?

She couldn't remember.

No, it wasn't the jockey. Constance had fixed her up with the jockey. Now, if that hadn't been a sight to behold. He was all of five-foot-two compared with her five-foot-ten inches in her stocking feet.

Of course, the guy had loved it. He'd strutted around like a rooster all evening.

Gracie had felt like shooting Constance that night. And if memory served her correctly, that was the day she'd sworn off dating altogether.

"Soft drink?"

She shook her head again. It was enough that he'd bought her ticket. This was all just very uncomfortable . . .

"Let's go get the good seats, Gracie." Izzie grabbed her hand and pulled her toward the guy who took their tickets. It was actually a relief to leave Carson behind gathering drinks and popcorn and Junior Mints for Izzie and himself.

But that relief was short-lived. Izzie found seats all right, front and center. They'd all have crooks in their necks in no time. Carson found them with no problem, though, and took the seat next to her. At first, Izzie was between them, but then she finagled her way to Carson's left, saying that it was easier for her to eat popcorn with her right hand. So, that left Carson and Gracie sitting side by side.

It still felt like a date.

It still felt damned uncomfortable.

Thank goodness the previews were coming on. At least she could just get engrossed in the movie and wouldn't have to communicate with him. At least they could just sit there. She didn't even have to eat his popcorn if she didn't want to.

That was one good thing about movies and dates.

But this wasn't a date, she reminded herself. Not in the least.

Even if it felt like it.

# TEN

Carson took a deep breath and expelled it slowly. Very slowly. He didn't want Gracie to hear the frustration in his sigh.

How in the hell had this happened?

This was supposed to be Izzie's day. Well, he supposed it still was. He *had* allowed his daughter to invite someone along. He just hadn't expected that that someone would be Gracie.

Not that he minded, actually; but it was going to be damned hard concentrating on anything other than the woman beside him all afternoon. Especially when he'd wanted to devote the time to his daughter.

Ever since last night, when he'd carried Gracie's lithe body upstairs, removed the shoes from her dainty feet, and brushed the silky strands of hair away from her face, he'd been more than captivated by his neighbor-slash-landlord. That something that had caught in his gut last night had yet to let go.

Of course, the pictures on her nightstand kept creeping back into his head, too. Especially the one with the man. She obviously loved the guy. But where was he? He and Gracie had been neighbors for several weeks now and he'd never seen the guy hanging around.

Come to think of it, there hadn't been any men around.

Hell, if he were Gracie's boyfriend, he'd be . . .

*Enough. Don't go there, Price.*

He stared at the screen.

Just as the dancing hot dogs and singing soft drinks jigged across the screen, Carson sidled a careful glance Gracie's way. With her right elbow resting on the chair arm, she was leaning into her hand, her fingers massaging her forehead and temples.

Without thinking, he leaned to his right and whispered, "Headache?"

Jerking upright, she dropped her hand and looked at him. A small wince crossed her face. "Yes."

"Aspirin?"

She shook her head. "Already consumed the limit," she whispered back.

Last night and this morning, he thought and inwardly chuckled. It wasn't funny, but he had the notion that Gracie Hart wasn't a regular boozer; so this was likely very uncharacteristic of her.

"I see. Soft drink? Caffeine can help a hangover." He pushed his toward her.

Her eyes grew wide and she shook her head. "No, thanks."

"I'll go get you one then."

"No, really. I don't want a soft drink."

"But—"

"Please, no." Her voice rose and her hand went to his arm. All Carson could do was stare at it. Her fingers and nails were just as graceful as the rest of her. Finally, he looked up into her face. Her eyes were pleading with him. Big, soft, doe-like eyes that twisted the wrench in his gut. Just a reminder, he guessed.

As if he needed a reminder that he found the woman extremely attractive.

But from her expression, he could tell that Gracie didn't want him to direct any more attention to the fact that she was severely hung over.

So, he didn't.

And as the hot dogs and soft drinks pirouetted off the screen, the lights went down and he couldn't see her face any longer.

He sat still for a moment, looking into the dark toward her. He discovered then that he didn't like not looking into her eyes.

"Dad, can we get ice cream?"

Gracie blinked painfully as they exited the theater, her eyes attempting to adjust to the unusually bright afternoon. Of course, her eyes were extremely sensitive today, so perhaps it was only her.

She glanced at Carson. He was squinting, too. Good. Maybe she was getting somewhat back to normal.

Carson looked back at her, appearing to assess something in her face. Then he turned his attention to Izzie. "Honey, I'm tired. How about if we do that later this evening?"

"But, Da-ad," Izzie whined. "We always get ice cream after a movie.

"Not today, Iz. Okay?"

"But Gracie wants to. Right, Gracie?"

"Well, uh . . ." she stammered.

He caught Gracie's eye again. Actually, she was tired herself, but should she let Carson handle this? She had the distinct feeling that he really didn't want to spend any more of his afternoon with her.

He'd been very quiet throughout the movie and once, when she'd accidentally crossed her legs and brushed her foot up against his calf, he'd jumped as if he were scared to death. Another time, his elbow had slipped off the armrest and his arm had fallen into her lap, startling both of them. Not to mention how he'd stared at her hand when she'd absentmindedly reached out and touched his arm.

She'd just make it easy on him.

"You two go," she interrupted. "I have some work to do back at the shop."

Izzie moved in front of Gracie, grasped her hand, and looked up at her with those huge Disney eyes. "Please, Gracie? Please? Don't go yet."

Heaving a deep sigh, she searched the child's eyes. Such an angelic little face. Reaching out, Gracie smoothed back a few wayward curls that had escaped her ponytail and smiled. Yet, she could be such a monkey. Starved for female attention, she'd deduced lately, this child was beginning to get to her. And bad.

Glancing up, Gracie searched Carson's face. But Izzie wasn't the only one getting to her. She'd known it for a while but had refused to acknowledge it. Carson was getting to her, too. She couldn't let that happen. Thing was, dad and kid were the whole kit-and-caboodle.

It was something she was just going to have to learn to deal with.

Stalling, she wracked her brain, wondering how she might manage to get an afternoon nap and appease Izzie at the same time.

Again, she looked down into the child's eyes. She saw life dancing in them. She saw a child so different from the one she'd been so many years ago. She saw spirit and spunk and an innocence she herself had lost long ago. She saw a childlike passion for living that radiated up at her with a zest Gracie had longed denied herself.

She saw exactly what she'd been missing for years, had not allowed herself to feel.

Love.

It was simple as that.

"How about this?" she whispered, crouching down to look Izzie directly in the eyes. The child smiled and continued to search her face. "I'm a little tired and your Dad is, too, I think. Why don't we all go home for the rest of the day today? Tomorrow, I'll get my old-fashioned ice cream freezer out and we'll make homemade ice cream out on the back deck. Deal?"

Izzie's face screwed up a bit. "You can make ice cream?"

"Yep. You never had homemade ice cream before?"

The monkey shook her head.

"Well. I think it's about time, don't you?"

Izzie smiled and nodded furiously. "But can't we do it today?"

Gracie shook her head. "I have some work to do and your father has to open up Geek's tonight, right?"

Looking up, Gracie finally allowed herself to glance back at Carson, who was staring at her with an odd expression on his face. Something abruptly clutched in her chest and she felt that she'd done something very wrong.

"I'm sorry," she said softly to him. "You may have had other plans for tomorrow. I should have—"

He put up his hand to stop her, his eyes not leaving hers. "No," he said. "We have no other plans. I think . . ." He paused and looked to his daughter, and Gracie followed his gaze. A long sigh exited his lips. Izzie, still clutching Gracie's hand, peered back at her dad with a most satisfied expression on her face. "I think," Carson continued, glancing back to Gracie now, "that we both would like that very much." Finally, a small, hesitant grin meandered across his lips.

For just a few seconds, Gracie studied his face. She found herself wanting to grin back. "Good," she returned softly, then finally allowed her lips to return the gesture.

Her heart suddenly felt full of something she didn't dare try to define, so she shoved it away. Far away. Trying not to acknowledge that that fullness felt good.

Too good.

The next afternoon, Gracie stared into her bathroom mirror and groaned. Her eyes were no longer red but they were still puffy.

She'd hoped that after she'd showered and gone to the grocery to gather ice cream supplies, and had drunk tons of water, the puffiness would have subsided.

No such luck. Small bags of puff still existed underneath each eye like little carpetbags of fluid.

Tea bags. That might do it. So after a few minutes, Gracie was lying in her bed with brewed and chilled tea bags on her eyes when she started wondering why she was even concerned about puffy eye-bags in the first place.

She wasn't trying to catch Carson Price's eye. She didn't need to look gorgeous for him. She didn't even *want* him to look at her in any way other than as his neighbor and landlord.

So what difference did it make if she had puffy eyes?

It didn't matter.

Quickly, Gracie rose and tossed the tea bags into the wastebasket in her bathroom. She splashed water on her face, toweled off, and didn't even look in the mirror before she left. She also acknowledged to herself that she hadn't put on a speck of makeup all day long.

What the heck. She was just going to make ice cream on her back deck with her neighbors. She didn't need makeup.

She didn't need to impress anyone. Least of all Carson Price. She just wanted to spend time with Izzie—and Izzie didn't care if she wore makeup or not.

She was in her kitchen some time later mixing up the ice cream ingredients when the knock came at her door.

"Door's open," she shouted, still stirring milk and eggs and sugar and vanilla and a few other things in a large mixing bowl.

The door burst open and like a whirlwind Izzie raced across her living room toward her small kitchen.

"Hey, Gracie!"

Gracie smiled. "Hey ya, monkey!"

"Whatcha doin'?"

"Getting ready to cook the ice cream."

"Cook it! But we gotta get it cold, not hot!" the imp exclaimed.

Smiling, Gracie transferred the mixture to a large saucepan. "Well, you have to cook this kind first, then we put it into the freezer to get cold and hard. It's going to take a little while, so I hope your mouth's not all set for ice cream just yet."

"How long?" she inquired.

"A few hours. But it will be worth the wait."

"Then just skip the cooking part." Izzie jumped up on a bar stool and peered across the snack bar into the mixture on the stove."

"Can't," Gracie explained. "This kind has eggs in t, and you have to cook the eggs so we don't get almonella."

"Simonhoola?"

Glancing up from her stirring, Gracie laughed. "Salmonella. It's a kind of food poisoning. In other words, if you get it, you throw up a lot."

"Samon-ellie?"

"Salmon . . . like the fish."

Izzie screwed up her face. "Cook it good, then, okay? I don't wanna puke like a fish."

Giggling, Gracie nodded and agreed. "Sure will, z."

As she glanced up, she noticed that her front door was still ajar and that Carson was standing in the door frame. Immediately, her heart clutched. How long he'd been there, she had no clue.

"May I come in?" he asked.

She nodded. "Of course."

Cautiously, he stepped across the threshold and toward the kitchen. After sidling up next to Izzie and depositing himself on another bar stool, he peered over to look at the mixture on the stove.

"You have to cook it?"

Gracie couldn't help but smile. "Yes," she told him, her attention still on the mixture. She turned the heat up a little bit.

"But we're going to freeze it, right?"

"It's 'cause you'll puke like a fish if she doesn't cook it," Izzie offered.

Gracie looked at Carson, who was looking at his daughter in surprise.

"You'll what?"

"You'll puke."

"Why?"

"Some fish thing."

Gracie chuckled and went back to her stirring.

"What fish thing?" Carson queried.

"The Simon fish thing."

"You mean, salmon, like salmon patties?"

"Yeah, like that."

"You're confusing me, Izzie. What does salmon have to do with ice cream?"

Izzie heaved out a sigh and tossed out her hands as she looked her dad square in the eyes. "It has to do with fish eggs. You have to kill them all. That's what makes you puke."

"Fish eggs," he echoed. Gracie felt his gaze on her, so she looked up.

"Fish eggs," she repeated and smiled.

"It's named after some girl named Simon Ellen," Izzie said then.

Carson guffawed and looked from Gracie to his daughter and back to Gracie again.

"Salmonella," she finally offered. "This recipe has eggs in it so, therefore, you have to cook it so you won't get salmonella."

"That's what makes you puke," Izzie explained.

Gracie laughed, still looking at Carson. "Yes, that's what makes you puke."

"Like a fish."

Again, Carson belted out a laugh. Leaning over, he bear-hugged Izzie and held her close. "You silly Munchkin," he told her. "I love your mind."

"I love your mind, too, Dad," Izzie chimed back.

Gracie suddenly realized she was smiling at the whole scene and had stopped stirring when a big *ker-plop!* bubbled up through the mixture.

"Oh, gosh!" Embarrassed, she turned down the heat and started furiously stirring. "Guess I need to pay attention to what I'm doing, huh?"

"Yep!" Izzie laughed.

"Please, do," Carson added. "Make sure you properly kill all those fish eggs."

"Or we have to tell Simon Ellen," Izzie told her.

Gracie continued stirring, laughter boiling up inside of her.

It was a nice feeling.

Carson swiped at his brow and continued cranking the arm of the old ice cream freezer. The swipe didn't help much; perspiration still dripped off his forehead onto the deck with huge plops. The July afternoon had turned into a humid evening. He wouldn't doubt that there was a summer thunderstorm in their near future.

"How much longer?" Izzie peered over his shoulder.

"Not too much, I think. It's getting harder to crank."

"That's good."

"Yes."

It was very good. His arm was tired. A few minutes passed and Izzie moved around to the front of him, intently watching the process.

"You're sweating, Dad."

"That I am, Iz."

"Is it hard?"

"You could say that." He glanced up. Where in the heck was Gracie? His arm was tired. No wonder she'd taken the first cranking shift. Surely this should be ready by now.

"Gracie's slicing strawberries."

Carson looked up at his daughter. "Why did you say that?"

"I saw you looking for her."

"No, I wasn't." He returned to his cranking. Water sloshed out of the drain hole.

"Yes, you were."

"Was not," Carson returned.

"Was too."

Frustrated, Carson stopped cranking and stared at his daughter. Slowly, he sat back on his heels, reached for his right bicep, and started rubbing the muscle. Who would have thought making home-made ice cream would be so much work?

"Was not," he countered and then threw her a narrowed gaze that meant *no more*. Besides cranking the freezer, his temper was bordering on cranky.

"Done yet?"

This was from Gracie, who just that second popped out the back door and stepped out onto the deck. She carried bowls and spoons and a plastic container which he hoped held those sliced strawberries. Perhaps all this cranking wouldn't be for naught.

"Not sure. How do you know?"

He watched as she set the dishes on the redwood table and approached the two of them. Smiling, she crouched down beside him and reached for the handle. After giving it one hard crank backward, she said, "Just a little longer."

"More?" he croaked.

"More," she replied.

"You're sure it's not done?"

"Positive."

He searched her eyes and realized that at some point today Gracie had added a touch of makeup to them. Her cheeks looked rosier, too. And she was wearing a hint of lipstick. She must be feeling better, he thought, and was glad about that.

"You're perspiring."

Chuckling, he reached for the hand-crank. "This is hard work!"

"But worth it."

He stopped midcrank and looked at her again. "Promise?"

Slowly, she nodded. "Promise. Now get cranking."

She walked away then and Izzie joined her. Carson found himself lost in the way she kidded with Izzie and gracefully moved about the deck and set the bowls and spoons and strawberries out on the table.

He was enjoying himself so much, he didn't even notice that his arm hurt like hell.

# ELEVEN

Twenty minutes later Carson lifted the last spoonful of creamy vanilla ice cream topped with a slice of just-ripe strawberry to his lips and savored the flavor, rolling it over on his tongue. The strawberry literally melted in his mouth along with the ice cream. He swallowed, then closed his eyes and leaned back on the padded redwood chaise lounge and sighed.

Heaven. Pure heaven.

"Good . . . huh, Dad?"

"Absolutely."

Carson opened one eye only to find the two females on the deck staring at him.

"Worth it?" Gracie asked.

"Yummy," he answered.

She grinned. "Told you so. More?"

Opening the other eye and sitting up, he told her no. "I've eaten more than my share already."

"But you did all the hard work," Gracie said. "You deserve more than the rest of us."

"Oh . . . I think you did the most important

vork," he replied. "I mean, killing those fish eggs
vas extremely important. Simon Ellen says so."

Gracie and Izzie looked at each other and burst
out laughing. Carson found that he immensely liked
the sound of their voices blended together in laugh-
er. But all too quickly Gracie stopped laughing and
rose to gather their bowls. She reached for his and
he handed it to her, holding onto the bowl just a
tad longer than he'd intended. Her fingertips
grazed his and their gazes briefly touched. A puzzled
look crossed Gracie's face and he let go of the bowl.
He couldn't deny, though, that he liked the electric
sizzle her touch had sent up his hand.

Quickly, she retrieved Izzie's bowl and set about
cleaning up other things. Carson rubbed his hand
on his leg to try to stop the sizzle. It wasn't working.

His daughter slowly made her way to where he
was sitting on the chaise and curled up in his lap.

"Sleepy, Munchkin?"

She yawned and nodded. "A little."

Glancing at his watch, Carson realized it was an
hour past her bedtime. Making the ice cream had
taken a lot longer than he'd expected. "Well, let's
help Gracie clean up; then we should get you to
bed."

He rose, taking the child with him. Izzie clung to
him, snuggling closer into her daddy's chest. Gracie
turned, her hands full of bowls and such.

"I can do this. Why don't you put her to bed?"
She smiled and Carson felt warm. Warmer than the
humidity and Izzie's hot body was making him. This
was something else entirely.

"I tell you what," he answered. "You do th
dishes, and as soon as I get her down, I'll come bac
and take care of the freezer, empty the ice, and hos
the salt off the deck. All right?"

Gracie must have liked the sound of that becaus
she actually smiled at him. "All right."

He liked the sound of that, too. It would give hin
one more chance today to be with her. He wasn'
sure why, but he felt compelled to spend a littl
more time with her. It was as if he needed to d
that, just to see if what was happening between then
was happening.

And to determine if he wanted what he though
was happening to really happen.

Something strange was happening between then
he was sure. Or maybe, it was just with him. Ther
was not a doubt in his mind: Gracie Hart was gettin
to him. And how.

He just wasn't sure that was a good thing.

Some time later Carson slipped through Gracie'
back door and joined her on the deck. The nigh
was cooling somewhat and the stars were sparklin;
overhead; an occasional drifting storm cloud hic
them from view. The day had been long and Graci
was tired, ready to relax. It had been a good day—
nice weekend, actually. For the first time in foreve
she'd given herself two full days off.

Night sounds skittered about, birds called, peopl
talked somewhere down the street, a cat meowed
She rested her head on the back of the chaise and

closed her eyes as she listened. Carson's footsteps
drew nearer. Then they paused and she heard the
creak of the redwood and knew he'd sat in the
chaise next to hers.

"She asleep?" Gracie asked, her eyes still closed.

"Finally," he answered after a minute.

"That's good."

"Yes."

Gracie thought about Izzie for a moment. "Don't
know how you do it sometimes."

When Carson didn't immediately answer, she
opened her eyes and turned toward him.

He was watching her intently.

"I love her."

Smiling, Gracie said, "I know. It's obvious." Then
she added, "She's a great kid, Carson. I like her a
lot."

"Even though she broke your crystal cookie
plate?"

"Even though." She grinned.

"I know sometimes she's a nuisance."

Gracie sat up and faced Carson. "No," she returned softly. "She's never a nuisance. I love having
her around. I hope you'll let her come over whenever she likes. I really enjoy her company."

Glancing away, she looked toward the sky to her
right. More clouds were tumbling in. An awkward
silence enveloped them.

"You're good with her," Carson finally said.

"She's good for me," she replied, looking back.

Carson placed his elbows on his knees and made
a tent with his fingers. Both of them were facing the

other, sitting on the sides of the lounges. He appeared to study her for a moment, as though he were contemplating asking her a question. Gracie simply studied him back, trying to anticipate his thoughts.

"I'm surprised you don't have children," he said.

At that, Gracie dropped her gaze. "Just one of those things," she said softly.

"Do you want children . . . someday?"

Lifting her gaze back to connect with his, she firmly replied, "Yes. More than anything. Someday." It startled her that she'd admitted that out loud. She hadn't talked with anyone lately about her obsession with having a child. Not even Constance or Amie.

"Difficult to plan those things sometimes, huh?"

Keeping the connection fully between them, Gracie smiled and replied softly, "Perhaps more than you realize."

They sat in silence. Then Gracie thought of something. "Carson, there's something you should know. I've kind of put off telling you."

He arched a brow. It was almost the eye thing and Gracie had to stifle a giggle. But she did, wanting to discuss something with him.

"What?"

She took a breath. "Izzie tossed a couple of water balloons out your apartment window onto Bets Baker the other night."

Gracie chewed the inside of her lip. Last thing she wanted to do was get Izzie into trouble, but she figured Carson had a right to know.

"She didn't," he said.

"She did."

He studied her for a moment. "Did she get her good?" A hint of a grin flashed across his lips.

Gracie clamped her lips between her teeth, not wanting to smile, and slowly nodded. "Afraid so. New hairdo, too."

Carson glanced off. "Well. I'll have to talk to her."

Gracie nodded. "You do that."

Then before she realized it, both of them burst into laughter. After a minute, Gracie had to hold her sides.

"It's really not funny," she told him.

"I know. I'm going to have to punish her."

"You should have seen Bets's face." Gracie giggled. "If she weren't so furious, she would have laughed herself."

Carson took a breath and tried to control himself. "I'm glad I didn't see it. It would be hard to keep a straight face while setting Izzie straight. That child." He shook his head and then looked back at Gracie. "Thanks for telling me. Please don't keep things like that from me. It's hard enough doing this parent thing on my own."

Gracie thought about that, her smile turning serious. She was sure what he said was the truth. "So, what about Izzie's mother, Carson? Does Izzie ever get to spend time with her?"

His expression took a sudden dive into seriousness, too. Shaking his head, he simply said, "No."

Gracie let it lie. A few moments later he added, "Izzie's mom and I divorced three years ago. She left us to pursue an acting career in California. She's not seen Izzie since. We've caught glimpses of her on commercials from time to time, and once in a while she calls or sends a gift. That's about the extent of it."

The mood had changed and Gracie realized that Carson was finished with that subject. She felt no need to pursue it further. Even though she knew she'd think about that for some time to come. Poor Izzie.

A clap of thunder sounded in the distance and each of them glanced toward the sound. A few seconds later a streak of lightning snaked across the sky.

"Cool front coming in," Carson offered. "Looks like it might storm. I'll get that freezer now." He stood and Gracie stood, too.

"I already took care of it."

"Oh?" He glanced about and sat back down again. So did Gracie. "I told you I would do it."

"I know. I just finished with everything else and it only took a minute."

Still sitting opposite her, Carson once again tented his fingers and Gracie continued to glance around, trying not to stare at him.

Thing was, she liked looking at him. Those eyes, which had caught her off guard from the very first time they'd met, mesmerized her each time his gaze took hold and held. Even small, skittering glances, where their gazes flitted and danced around one another, caught her in a web of enchantment and made her only want to stare into them all the more.

"May I ask you a question?"

Carson nodded slowly. "Sure."

"Was it you who tucked me into bed the other night?"

Again their gazes locked and Gracie was determined not to let hers skitter away this time. The question had rattled through her mind for two days. She needed to know.

Finally, he dropped his chin in a nod. "Yes," he replied in a low voice. "Your friends sort of abandoned you and I was left to the task."

A task. Now she was a task.

"Ah. I see." Her gaze skittered then.

"Not that I minded, however."

"Oh."

"I think your friends planned it, though."

Gracie frowned. The little matchmakers. "I wouldn't put it past them. I apologize."

Shaking his head, he replied, "Don't apologize." Then his voice lowered, became soft. "I told you, I didn't mind."

Gracie looked back at him. He looked questioningly into her eyes. She wasn't quite sure what she should say back to that. A small shiver snaked down her spine and she had to really concentrate not to let her whole body shiver. "Well . . . thank you for taking care of me," she said finally. "I'm not quite sure what came over me that evening. It's actually . . . uh, it was a little embarrassing. I, uh, usually don't do things like that."

A smile cracked Carson's face. "I know that. No need to be embarrassed." His smile broadened then. "You were pretty darned cute, you know."

Suddenly, Gracie felt hot and flushed. "Well, gee, if I'd known before now that I was a cute drunk, I'd have done it long ago."

Chuckling, Carson dropped his hands and stood. In one movement, he covered the distance between them and sat beside Gracie on the lounge chair. "Well, as cute as you were, I really don't think it's you."

Gracie bit her lip. "You know, I don't think it's me, either."

They sat for a minute, thunder still gently rolling in the background, studying the stars. Gracie studied Carson's profile while he looked to the sky. A moment later, he slowly turned toward her, leaned closer, and—before she knew it—had touched his lips to hers in a soft, slow kiss.

It was only a brief kiss but very sweet. When Gracie opened her eyes, she saw Carson staring back at her. Her heart pounded then and she wasn't quite sure she was breathing.

A moment of silence fell between them and then Carson spoke. "Mind if I ask you a question?" he said softly.

Gracie continued to study his face, her heart fluttering. "No. I don't mind."

He glanced away for several seconds then turned back to her. "When I tucked you into bed the other night, I couldn't help but notice the photos on your lamp table. I thought you might tell me about them."

Gracie was stunned. That question came from way out in left field and there was no way she was prepared for it. That small kiss and her wonder as to why he kissed her were all but forgotten. Hesitantly, she pushed away, stood, and walked toward the edge of the deck, facing out over the parking lot. Several minutes passed and she didn't answer him.

She didn't know how to answer him. She rarely talked about it with anyone. And if she did talk about it, it was with Amie or Constance, who were both women and understood. She'd never once discussed it with a man. At least not a man she was attracted to.

"I'm sorry. I guess it's personal. I shouldn't have asked."

She heard Carson rise and step toward her back door. Turning, she watched as he reached for the doorknob.

"Which picture do you want to know about?" she called out softly. It was an impromptu decision, but she was glad once she'd blurted it out. For some reason, she didn't want him walking away. Not yet.

He stopped and turned, dropping his hand to his side. His gaze met hers again and suddenly she wanted to tell him something. Perhaps not all and definitely not every detail. But something.

"The one of you," he told her quietly, "as a ballerina."

From somewhere deep inside, she mustered up the words. "Ten years ago, I was a ballet dancer. In New York. For five years of my life. I studied as a child. It was all I ever wanted to do." It was more than she'd planned on telling him.

"But you don't do it anymore?"

She shook her head.

"Why?"

"It's . . . complicated."

"I'd like to hear."

"Someday, maybe. Not now."

Nodding, he conceded and paused before he asked, "And the other picture?" She had a feeling that was the one he was more interested in knowing about. Did he think she had a lover somewhere? Did that bother him?

Gracie lifted her chin and again called upon that ball of courage deep in her gut to find the words. "He was my fiancé," she simply said.

Carson swallowed and stared at her. "Key word being was."

"Yes."

"So, he's not your fiancé anymore?"

"No," she replied.

"What happened?"

Gracie felt the tears beginning to sting the backs of her eyelids, so she decided to get this over with as quickly as possible.

"He died," she told him. "The same night my ballet career died."

Then not wanting to discuss any of it further, she quietly stepped around him and escaped to the solitude of her apartment. Where she belonged.

Her dreams that night were laced with confused visions of her lost love and feelings of hope as the warmth of Carson's brief kiss invaded her dreams.

\* \* \*

The next evening Gracie sat near the center of her bed, Izzie cross-legged in front of her, Claire curled up in a ball in Izzie's lap, and Bandit chewing on an old shoe at the foot of her bed.

Reaching out, Gracie gently grasped another strand of Izzie's hair and ran a brush over it. Continuing to brush the child's long curls, Gracie found herself smiling. Brushing Izzie's hair was soothing and relaxing and she enjoyed it very much. Just bathed and dressed in her pajamas, Izzie smelled of powder and soap. The hair closest to her scalp was slightly damp, she noticed, the result of running bath water up to her chin.

It was a pleasant and contented scene and Gracie was immensely enjoying herself. Claire was quite satisfied being the receiver of Izzie's ministrations and Bandit was happy just to chew.

Gracie was happy just to have Izzie for the evening. The child had bathed in her tub, bubbles and all, while Gracie had pampered her as a little six-year-old girl should be pampered. Well, she might have even gone overboard just a tad.

She'd lit some aromatherapy candles in the bathroom and burned some incense while a favorite classical piece played low in the background. She'd even allowed Izzie to soak in the tub and drink a flute of Sprite while she bathed.

The child had looked so cute, her hair all piled on her head, bubbles up to her chin, the crystal flute dangling from her fingertips, black smudges still on her face from where she'd crawled under the deck earlier.

She was spoiling the child, she knew. But she also knew that Izzie needed girlie things—even if she thought she didn't want girlie things. And Gracie needed to give her girlie things.

She'd worked hard all day and was immensely glad to be able to relax with Izzie. Hard work and concentrating on the child kept her mind off the one thing it kept wanting to drift to all day long. Carson.

Their conversation the night before had dredged up the nightmares of her past. Her sleep had been interrupted with faces and images and she hadn't slept well. But worse than that were the images of Carson's face that had popped into her head all day long, along with the phrases he'd used the night before, which made her wonder just where his thoughts were leading.

She was confused. Not only about him, but about how she felt for him.

"Do you think I should cut my hair?" Izzie asked then, startling her from her musings.

"No!" Gracie answered quickly, diverting her attention back to the child. "Why would you think of cutting this beautiful hair?"

"It gets in my way. I was thinking I'd like it better cut like a boy's."

"Oh, Izzie, it's beautiful! You don't want to cut it. Besides, it's all grown out now and you can simply put it in a ponytail if it gets in your way. When it's shorter and growing out, you can't do that."

"I know. That's what Daddy said."

"Well, your Daddy is right."

"Her Daddy is right about what?"

Gracie looked up, startled that Carson had entered her bedroom. Evidently, from the look on his face, he was startled that she was startled.

"I knocked; I guess you two didn't hear me. The door was open, so I just thought I'd step on in . . ."

Gracie waved her hand and smiled trying to act nonchalant. "No, don't be silly. Of course it's all right."

This was the first she'd seen of Carson all day; and even though it was a little unnerving to have him step into her bedroom, she tried to act relaxed—for Izzie's sake. She'd felt a little guilty that she hadn't given him a chance to further discuss her ballet career or Evan's death last night. She'd quickly bid him good night and slipped inside her back door, leaving him alone on the deck.

The storm had blown in a few minutes later.

Gracie rather liked, and was thankful for, the pounding of the rain and the howling of the winds against her windows. It made her tears and emotions feel all the less significant. She'd cried herself to sleep last night, unsure of whether she was sad about her past or the uncertainty of her future.

Both bothered her. Both were difficult for her to get a handle on.

"Izzie was asking me about getting her hair cut," she finally said to Carson.

"And you told her no, right?"

Allowing a grin, she nodded. "I told her her hair was too beautiful to cut and that a ponytail should still work just fine for her right now."

Carson nodded in agreement. "Thanks." He shuffled from one foot to the other. "Do you mind tucking her in for me tonight? We've got a big birthday crowd coming in a few minutes downstairs and I might not be able to get away when I'd like."

Gracie shook her head. "Of course not. You know I don't mind. We can leave the doors ajar and I can hear her if she needs me."

Izzie jumped up on her knees. "Can I stay with Gracie tonight, Daddy? She has an extra room."

Carson shook his head. "Izzie, you don't invite yourself."

"She won't care."

"But that's not the point, Iz. Besides, you and I have to get up very early in the morning to go to Louisville. Gracie might not want to get up that early. I think you should just stay in your bed tonight, and perhaps, if you are invited, we can consider that for another time."

Ever the negotiator, Gracie was reminded of Carson's former law profession. She supposed those skills might have some merit in parenting, too.

"But, Dad . . ."

"Iz."

The child frowned, but knew her father's warning face. "Okay."

He motioned for her, and in the next instant she flew from the bed and into her father's arms. Gracie watched as a disturbed Claire arched her back, then stretched, then yawned and curled herself into the dent on the bed where Izzie had been sitting. Bandit was now nipping at Carson's ankles.

"Give me a kiss."

She did and he sat her back on the bed. Turning to Gracie, he said, "You're sure you don't mind?"

"Not at all. Anytime."

Carson grinned hesitantly, then stepped toward the door. "I'll check with you later, Gracie. Night, Munchkin. Bandit! Quit nipping at my heels!"

Laughing, Gracie watching him leave, suddenly wondering why things between them had gotten so much easier the past few days.

Or had they?

# TWELVE

Gracie woke with a start.

Groggily, she turned her head to the side and listened. She'd heard something, but what? Unsure, she sat quietly in her chair, fished the remote control out of her lap, and turned off the television. She must have fallen asleep while watching the news.

Maybe it was the television. Maybe that's what she'd heard. Or the cat.

*"Mom-my!"*

It wasn't the cat.

The child's scream echoed through the stairwell and into Gracie's living room. Like a gunshot, she bolted from her chair and raced from her apartment and into the one next door, scrambling through the rooms until she reached Izzie.

The child was crying and moaning. Curled into a ball and clutching her wadded-up blanket close to her heart, Izzie moved from side to side, whimpering. "Mommy," she said again, then she took some shallow breaths and sobbed.

Gracie's heart broke into pieces. She rushed to Izzie and gathered her close.

"Izzie," she whispered. "It's okay. I'm here." She held the child close and rocked her. "It's Gracie. Wake up, honey; you're having a bad dream."

Besides breaking, her heart went out to the child. Her cries for her mommy were nearly Gracie's undoing, and soon she found tears in her own eyes. She knew then, at that moment, that should she ever become a mommy, nothing on this planet would keep her from seeing to her child's every need or from being with her child when she needed her.

How Izzie's mother could walk away from her only child for her career, she would never understand. As much as Gracie loved ballet, she'd always known that when her first child came along, her career would go on the back burner.

For that matter, she couldn't understand how Izzie's mother could walk out on Carson, either. She'd left her entire family. The thought was not plausible. All Gracie had ever wanted in her life, besides ballet, was a husband and a family. It had been snatched away from her before she'd ever gotten it. Carson's wife had had everything, and had casually walked away.

She'd never understand it.

"Gracie?" the child's weakened voice came to her.

"Yes, honey. I'm here."

"Hold me tighter."

"I am, Munchkin." Gracie stroked damp stray hairs from Izzie's temple.

She'd never before used Carson's nickname, but

tonight it felt right. Maybe Izzie needed that familiarity right now.

"You okay?" she whispered a few moments later.

Izzie nodded and snuggled closer. Gracie brought the blanket around them both and settled back against the pillows with her. "Bad dream," Izzie said then.

"I'm sorry," Gracie whispered. "I hope I made it go away."

Izzie was quiet for a while. Her face was still in Gracie's chest, so she couldn't tell if the child was fully awake or not. After a minute, she nodded against her.

"It was my mommy. She kept running away."

Gracie winced. She was beginning to despise Izzie's mommy. "Maybe she didn't see you."

"She saw me. She kept running . . . and I kept running . . . I couldn't catch her . . . and then she disappeared."

Gracie held her tighter.

"I wish you were my mommy," Izzie said sleepily and yawned. "You wouldn't run away, would you?"

Gracie couldn't think of a response. There was no way she could ever go there, ever think anything remotely close to that or encourage the child to think that that could happen. Last thing she needed was Izzie thinking that the possibility that she could become her mommy could exist.

Because it couldn't.

"How about if I be your best friend?" she offered quietly. "Best friends don't go away."

Izzie must have been thinking about that. "Joey Brockman is my best friend."

Gracie smiled. "How about if I be your best *girl* friend."

She thought a little longer. "Okay," she finally said.

Gracie snuggled further beneath the covers with Izzie. They were quiet for some time. Izzie's breathing became slow and even and Gracie wondered if she'd gone back to sleep. She held her, thinking again about all that Izzie's mother was missing out on.

"My mother is a famous actress, you know."

Gracie had thought Izzie was asleep. "She is?"

"Yes. And someday she'll come visit and take me to California where they make the movies."

"She will?" It was hard for Gracie to follow Izzie's irrational thinking. But then again, she was a child and had awakened from a restless sleep.

"Ummmhmmmm . . ."

"So you'd like to do that?"

Izzie nodded against her chest. "Uh-huh."

"Bet your daddy would miss you."

Izzie sighed. "Oh, he'd come, too. Someday, my daddy and my mommy will get married again."

This time Gracie sighed. "Oh." Try as she might, reminding herself that Izzie was practically talking in her sleep, Gracie still couldn't stop the pang that pierced her stomach at that statement.

"Ummhmmm . . ."

"Really?"

"Yeah. My daddy told me . . ."

Izzie relaxed and very quickly fell back to sleep. With her arms wrapped around the child like a protective cocoon, Gracie was afraid to move, fearful she'd wake her again. She decided to stay put, her mind drifting over their conversation. Not wanting to think too much about Izzie's mommy and daddy getting back together. Blessedly, all too quickly, she found herself drifting into sleep, the conversation just a myriad of thoughts meandering through her mind.

When Carson stepped inside Izzie's bedroom sometime later that evening, the scene that met him was not the one he'd expected. He'd expected to find a sleeping Izzie, sheets and covers all in disarray, her head at the foot of the bed and her feet on her pillows, with Bandit tucked up under her chin asleep. That was Izzie's normal sleeping position. Most nights he'd gently turn her around and tuck her in, only to find by morning that she'd somehow twisted herself back to the foot of the bed again.

But tonight—tonight he met with something entirely different. From out of nowhere, a huge lump formed in his throat and he was having a helluva time swallowing.

Gracie was there.

Tucked in beside Izzie, their heads actually pillowed against the headboard, the sheets and covers neatly pulled up around them, Gracie slept with Izzie cradled in her arms. Izzie's head rested on Gracie's shoulder. The fingers of Gracie's right hand were curled loosely against his daughter's cheek as though she'd fallen asleep brushing wayward curls away from her face. Bandit and Claire slept wrapped around each other next to Izzie.

He had to chuckle at that.

Carson hated to wake any of them. It was after 2:00 A.M. and he was tired, too. His night had been long. The crowd downstairs had been loud, along with the music and the pinging of the arcade games. He had half a notion to shove the animals aside and curl up next to his daughter and the woman next door who had somehow invaded every single one of his thoughts the past few days.

He was sorely tempted.

But he wouldn't do it.

Still, he didn't want to leave. Careful not to wake them, he sat on the edge of the bed. His thigh grazed Gracie's. The blanket covered her, but he could feel the sensation of her touch through the blanket and the warmth of her flesh.

He wanted to be next to her. That primal urge was boiling up from somewhere deep inside him and no matter how much he told himself that he didn't want a relationship, that he didn't need a woman in his life, the urge to share something with Gracie was almost more than he could fathom.

Watching her with Izzie this past weekend had been pleasant. Very pleasant. It was almost healing. At times, it reminded him of what he'd once had with Marci. It made him long for that again. But more than that, it reminded him of what he'd always wanted. Family.

But the scene before him was becoming too cozy, perhaps. Too much for Izzie to handle. Maybe too much for him to handle.

Although he liked having Izzie spend time with Gracie, he was almost afraid she was getting too close to their neighbor. What would happen if, for some reason, Gracie didn't want to be in Izzie's life any longer?

He frowned at the thought. For multiple reasons. Some he didn't even want to explore or acknowledge.

Gracie sighed and he lifted his gaze to watch the even rise and fall of her chest. She was wearing the same nightshirt from some time back, he noticed. The one she'd had on when Izzie had fallen down the stairs. Problem was, he also remembered exactly what she looked like in that nightshirt, even though he could only see a small glimpse of it peeking out from beneath the covers.

Closing his eyes, he recalled the image before him as she'd stood on the steps that day. Painted toenails, long legs, and all.

He sighed and opened his eyes again.

Izzie whimpered and rolled away from Gracie. Her arms slack now, Gracie didn't hamper the child's movement. Izzie rolled closer to the animals. Bandit snorted and turned belly up; Claire remained still, an unmovable lump of softly snoring sleeping fur.

Leaning over Gracie, Carson carefully attempted to reposition the covers over his daughter. She was out like a light. He tucked and moved closer to kiss her lightly on the cheek. Izzie whimpered again and he lingered, watching his daughter's slumber.

Slowly, he moved back to the side of the bed. A quick remembrance of several nights earlier raced through his mind as he brought the covers up around Gracie. No use in her getting cold in the night either, he reasoned.

But he remained next to her as he had once before, so tempted to reach out and smooth baby-fine hairs away from her temples, as she'd done for his daughter earlier. As he'd done a few nights ago for her.

Her breathing was even and shallow, her lips slightly parted. Suddenly, Carson's thoughts were no longer on smoothing the hair away from her face, but on the softness of Gracie's lips and how they might feel, once again, pressed against his.

And in the next instant, he found out.

Gracie woke to a gentle wheezing in her ear.

Forcing one eyelid open, she squinted as the morning sun shining through her window was filtered through something fuzzy and lumpy to her right.

Wait a minute, she thought. I don't get the morning sun in my bedroom window.

Rising up on one elbow, she opened the other eye and glanced around her.

This wasn't her room. This was Izzie's room.

Ah . . . she remembered now. The nightmare.

But Izzie wasn't still in bed with her. She was nowhere to be found. Claire, however, was still sleeping soundly beside her. Gracie was surprised that the cat hadn't wakened her long ago, wanting to be fed. Claire must have been the something fuzzy blocking some of the morning sun from her face a minute earlier. The wheezing something fuzzy.

Now how in the world had she ended up sleeping here all night?

Falling back on a pillow, Gracie tried to recall the scene from the night before.

Izzie had screamed. She'd groggily rushed next door to see what was the matter. The child had had a nightmare involving her mother. And Gracie had fallen asleep wondering what kind of mother would leave a child like Izzie.

Yes, she did vaguely remember falling asleep in Izzie's bed.

But then, there was something else, wasn't there?

She closed her eyes, trying to recall.

A dream. Had to have been. She'd had a dream of her own.

But it wasn't a nightmare, although it was quite confusing. And nice. Scary even. But still nice.

Sometime in the night, she'd dreamed Carson had kissed her. Again.

"Gracie's sleeping late."

"No, we're up early."

"But she's usually up by now."

"How do you know that?"

" 'Cause I hear her shower running while I'm still in bed every morning."

Carson thought about that. The kid was perceptive. And she was right. He'd lain in bed on numerous occasions and heard Gracie's shower running next door. Of course, he didn't care to think for long about Gracie in the shower. Particularly after the stupid thing he'd done last night.

"Are we just going to leave her in my bed?"

Carson put Izzie's half-eaten bowl of cereal down the garbage disposal. "Yes." He ushered her toward the door, trying to ignore thoughts about Gracie in any bed. "We'll leave her a note. You ready?"

Izzie stopped and placed her hands on her hips. "But what if she wakes up and is scared 'cause she's in a strange place."

Carson sighed. "Gracie is a big girl, Munchkin. She'll be fine. Besides, Claire is with her. So, grab Bandit and let's go."

Izzie planted herself into the carpet. "I don't wanna."

"But I wanna. We've got to get to Louisville. C'mon now." He opened the front door and motioned her through the door.

"I'll stay here with Gracie," she told him.

"No. You're coming with me. Remember, Kate is expecting you."

"I know, but—"

"Don't you want to see Kate?"

"Yes, but—"

"Then let's get going."

She shook her head. "No."

Carson couldn't believe his ears. His child was telling him no?

He glared at her. "Isabella, this isn't up for negotiation. I have to be in Louisville in one hour. I'm already pushing it. Kate is expecting you for the day. Now, grab the pup and let's vamoose."

Izzie glared back at him. Slowly, she bent to pick up the dog, held him in her arms, looked hesitantly at her father, but still didn't move. "I wanna stay with Gracie today."

Hell. He didn't have time for this. "You're spending the day with Kate. You can spend time with Gracie some other time. Besides, Gracie has to work."

"But she's still in bed."

"And we're letting her sleep."

"I'll wake her and she'll let me stay."

"No, she was up late. We'll let her sleep."

"I was up late, too, but you didn't let me sleep. I had a really bad nightmare."

Carson huffed out a breath. Izzie had told him all about the nightmare during breakfast. The fact that it involved Marci might have something to do with his foul mood. He was just glad, and thankful, that Gracie had been there for her. "That's because Kate is expecting you."

"Call her."

"No."

"Kate doesn't braid my hair like Gracie."

"Well, neither do I, but you stay with me."

"Kate makes chocolate milk funny."

Carson eyed his daughter. "Let me guess. And Gracie makes it just right, right?"

"Yep."

He shook his head and, with every passing word, was getting more determined to get his daughter out of the house and back with Kate for the day. Izzie was definitely getting too dependent on Gracie. "Well, I'm sorry about that, but you're going with me."

"But Gracie lets me play with her jewelry and Kate never lets me do stuff like that."

"I thought you didn't like girlie stuff."

"I don't."

"Then why?"

"I just like to."

"Gracie—"

"No!"

"But—"

"It's only for the day, Iz."

"Please, Daddy?"

"Isabella! I said no!"

Carson had raised his voice entirely too loudly and he was quite certain that he'd probably awakened Gracie. Damn. He had to get the child out the door before she stepped through the bedroom door.

Then Gracie stepped through the bedroom door.

"Why did you let me sleep?"

"Gracie!" Izzie ran toward her and wrapped her arms around her waist. Smiling groggily, Gracie enveloped the child in her arms.

"Good morning, Izzie. Guess I slept in your bed last night, huh?"

"Yeah." The child was grinning from ear to ear. Carson didn't like it.

"Izzie, c'mon. We have to go. Gracie, I'm sorry to leave so quickly, but I have an appointment this morning with my former law partner. A case we need to finish up. Gotta go." He reached out to grasp Izzie's arm.

She nodded, understanding. He wished she'd wrapped a sheet around her or something. That damned t-shirt was not what he needed to see this morning.

"Since Gracie's up, I'll just stay here, Dad."

"No." He gave Izzie the warning stare.

"Dad, don't do that eye thing at me, okay?" she responded.

"I'm not doing the eye thing, Izzie."

"Not *that* eye thing Dad, but the other one. The one where you try to look mean at me."

Carson was just about tired of this whole ordeal. "Isabella, pick up the dog and let's go. Now."

"She can stay with me if you'd like, Carson. It's not a problem."

*Oh, yes, it is a problem. More than you know.*

Carson shot his gaze to Gracie. Not her, too. Damned females. He blew out a breath. "Thank you, Gracie, but no. I've already made plans for Izzie today and, quite frankly, this is one time she's not going to get her way. So . . . please, just let me take care of this, all right?"

As soon as the words were out of his mouth, he realized he'd spoken much too harshly. In the next instance, that observation was written all over her face.

"Of course. I wouldn't dream of interfering," she bit out.

Carson knew she was puzzled, maybe even angry, but right now he didn't have time to think about it. Feeling even more guilty because he knew she'd helped him out last night, he tried to shake off what he was feeling.

Later. He'd just have to deal with it later.

He looked to his daughter. "Izzie, now."

She picked up Bandit, screwed her mouth into a tight little bow, knitted her brows, and stomped through the door and down the steps. He glanced behind her, then turned toward Gracie.

"I'm sorry. She was just being so—"

"It's not a problem," she told him sharply, shaking her head and waving him off. "Go. You'll be late. I can see my way out."

Carson hesitated, feeling that maybe he needed to say something else, then he decided to just let it be and left her standing there.

But at the door, he turned and faced Gracie again. "Thank you for watching her last night. And for being with her. Izzie told me about the nightmare."

The look on Gracie's face softened. "You're welcome. I'm glad I was there."

Carson nodded, realizing that once again, he hadn't been there when his daughter needed him. Seemed no matter what he did, he just couldn't change that scenario.

A funny feeling snaked over him all the way to Louisville. It took him awhile to shake it. But by the

time he'd arrived at his law office, he'd figured out
what it was.

And, he'd figured out what he needed to do about
it, too.

Or, at least he hoped he had it figured out.

# THIRTEEN

"Grace Elizabeth Hart, that outfit will never do."

Dumbfounded, Gracie looked down at herself and then stared at Amie. What was wrong with her new ivory blouse, made of a replication of hand-spooled Brussels bobbin lace, and her mauve ankle-length skirt?

"Why?"

"Because it just won't, that's why. This is a cocktail party, not a Victorian tea."

Gracie scowled. "Whatever are you talking about, Amie? I'm definitely not dressed for an afternoon tea party. This outfit is fine. Now let's go."

"No, it's not. And we're not leaving until you change."

Gracie huffed out a breath and rolled her eyes. She slammed her purse down on the counter next to her cash register and, hands on hips, turned to her friend. "I believe that I've been dressing myself for quite some time and I believe that I know the appropriate attire to wear to an evening function.

My goodness, this is Franklinville, for goodness sake, not New York City."

"Well, perhaps you should dress as if it's New York City."

What Amie was getting at, Gracie had no clue. Her attire was fine. She'd actually bought it in Boston on her trip a few weeks earlier.

"It's a hospital fund-raiser, Amie. It's the country club. I'll be fine."

Amie glanced at her watch. "We have time. And besides, Constance isn't here yet. I told her we'd meet her here at the shop. Now go change! I'm sure you have a little black dress up there somewhere. Try that."

Not a second later, the bell above the door chimed. In walked Constance. "Let's go," Gracie said, grabbing her purse. She'd had just about all she wanted to listen to about her clothing.

Constance took one look at her and stopped in her tracks. "Oh, Gracie. That outfit will never do."

Resisting the urge to scream, Gracie took two more steps toward the door. "I'm fine. Let's go."

Constance blocked the doorway.

Gracie stared her in the eyes.

Amie brought up the rear.

"The outfit," Constance said, "has to go."

And before she knew it, both Amie and Constance had hooked their arms in hers and were leading her through the store, up the back stair, and into her apartment and bedroom.

They released her and Gracie plopped on her bed with a *humph*. "The two of you are crazy," she muttered while they rifled through her closet. "My skirt and blouse are fine. This is what I'm wearing."

Amie popped a little black dress from the closet. "There. This will do nicely."

"It's too short," Gracie replied, inspecting her nails.

"It will be lovely," Constance told her while fishing a pair of black heels from her closet. "These are perfect."

Amie went to Gracie's jewelry box. "The pearls are all you'll need, honey." She placed them on the dressing table. "Necklace and earrings. Now, we'll move along so you can change." She ushered Constance toward the door. "Toodles!"

Tossing her a high finger-wave and a mischievous smile, Amie left the bedroom right after Constance. Gracie wasn't quite sure what in the hell had transpired the past few minutes.

She glanced down at herself. There was absolutely nothing wrong with how she was dressed. Nothing!

She was fine.

Absolutely fine.

Nothing would convince her otherwise.


He was about to leave until he caught sight of Gracie.

The cocktail party to top off a day of fund-raisers for the local hospital was a bit much for him. Besides playing in the golf tournament that afternoon, he'd been up early that morning helping with the pancake breakfast. All in all, he'd had a day of it and was ready to call it a night.

Until Gracie stepped through the country club doors and changed his mind.

He couldn't take his eyes off her.

And if he'd managed for one second *to* take his eyes off her, he imagined he'd see every other set of male orbs in the placed glued to her as well.

But he didn't risk it. He couldn't look away.

Gracie was stunning.

And he . . . well . . . he was stunned.

He'd watched her flip pancakes all morning at Amie's for the benefit breakfast while he played waiter and cleaned tables. He'd caught sight of her several times that afternoon serving up drinks and snacks at the concession stand during the golf tourney. But he'd yet had a chance to talk to her today. He wondered if she was still miffed at him.

But he'd be damned if he'd wait any longer.

As he slowly made his way toward her, he felt his heart begin a steady thrum in his chest. She was chatting with someone else—he had no clue to whom because his eyes were only for her.

The black dress . . . he could only suck in his breath and hold it . . . the effect it had on him was mind-boggling. Not that he hadn't seen women in little black dresses before. He's seen them hundreds of times.

But he'd never seen Gracie in a little black dress. He'd never seen any woman do a little black dress justice the way she did. It clung to every curve of her tall, lithe dancer's body and moved with every gesture she made. It was short. Shorter than any other dress he'd ever seen her wear. But not so short it was indecent. It was . . . just right.

A single strand of pearls graced her neck. Matching pearl stud earrings pierced her lobes. He drew closer and could see their luster from the overhead lights.

Perfect.

Simple, sophisticated beauty.

That was Gracie. Simply Gracie.

His Gracie.

It was at that moment he knew that he loved her. He stopped in his tracks, and his thoughts didn't go any further than that. He wouldn't let them. Not tonight.

He was simply in love with Gracie Hart. And he didn't plan to leave her side until she was ready to walk out the door with him tonight.


Agnes Branson was boring her to tears.

Gracie tried to stifle the yawn she felt coming on, but still had to hide it behind her fingertips. She had no clue what the woman was saying—although she needed to hear what Agnes was saying. As the hospital fund-raising chairperson, Agnes had been in charge of the day's events. Gracie nodded and hoped she hadn't volunteered for some future thing. You never knew with Agnes. She was tricky.

Exhausted from the day, she wished she'd just skipped this evening affair. She was about to yawn again, planning her means of early escape, when someone touched her elbow. Turning toward the person next to her, Gracie forgot anything about Agnes within the second.

Carson was at her elbow.

A delicious-looking Carson all decked out in suit and tie, all spit-shined and polished.

My goodness, she thought, he's a good-looking man. Her heart did that thing that she'd avoided for so long. It fluttered like crazy. And she let it. Wanted it.

"Good evening, Gracie," he said, the words rolling like warm honey off his lips.

She smiled slightly. "Hi, Carson."

He let out a deep sigh and didn't say anything else for a moment. Gracie waited. "You look very lovely this evening," he finally said.

Feeling her cheeks flush, Gracie glanced down at herself, then smiled as she looked Carson in the eyes again. Damn but she hated to admit it—perhaps Amie and Constance had been right. "Thank you," she replied softly. "You're looking mighty handsome yourself."

Carson chuckled. "Thanks."

Agnes cleared her throat, calling Gracie's attention back to the older woman. "Call me about that date in October, Gracie?" she said.

Nodding, Gracie told her she would. Finally, the woman left.

This time it was Gracie who let out the sigh. Looking back to Carson, she said, "I think I just volunteered for something. I have no clue what it was."

"Uh-oh. That could be dangerous." He laughed

again and Gracie agreed with him. "May I get you a glass of wine or something?" he offered.

Gracie glanced toward the bar. "You know, I was thinking earlier about a glass of wine, but I was afraid it might put me right to sleep. I'm suddenly feeling exhausted."

"Then how about if we grab a glass of wine and head out of here for a relaxing drive home. I was about to make my exit when I saw you come in."

Gracie studied him for a moment. "You were?"

"Yeah, dead on my feet."

"Same here. Why didn't you go?"

"Saw you. Thought maybe . . . hell . . . thought maybe you'd like to come with me. I'd like a little peace and quiet for a while. How about you?"

It didn't take long for Gracie to respond. "Let's do it."

And Carson didn't give her long to reconsider. After leading her to the bar and grabbing two glasses of wine, he escorted her out the back and into the parking lot.

Gracie hadn't felt this carefree in years.

Carson didn't want to go home. The country club sat about seven miles from town on a winding country road. The night was still, stars were bright in the sky, and the temperature was a perfect seventy degrees. As they approached his Corvette, he turned to Gracie.

"Mind if I put the top down?" It seemed like a

perfect night to him, but he wasn't sure if she would like it.

"Can we drink wine and drive with the top down at the same time?"

Smiling, he looked at her. "You drink your wine while I put the top down. In fact, take mine. I'm not sure I want it now."

He handed Gracie his glass. "This could be a mistake," she said, taking it and smiling back.

"Don't worry. I'll take care of you."

Gracie looked intently into Carson's eyes and he noticed the puzzled expression there. He knew she was an independent woman who was used to taking care of herself. Why he'd said that to her, he didn't know. But for some reason, he felt that maybe, just for tonight, she needed to be taken care of. For a fleeting moment, he worried that he'd said the wrong thing.

"Okay," she said. "I may have to hold you to that." She sipped at her glass of wine, hesitated a moment, then tipped it up and drained the glass. "One down."

She smiled the broadest smile then and Carson felt his heart do a flip-flop in his chest.

Turning, he grinned just as broadly, although she couldn't see it. As he started working on the Corvette, he had the strangest feeling this might be an interesting evening.


Gracie wasn't quite sure when she'd felt so relaxed. Wind blowing through her hair, which had long since come loose of its clip, soft music from the stereo, stars twinkling overhead, and the effects of two downed glasses of wine had made her sufficiently mellow.

They weren't anywhere near Franklinville, Gracie knew. Carson had suggested it was a nice evening for a drive and she hadn't protested. In fact, this was quite nice. Extremely nice.

"I'm glad you suggested this," she said, her head leaning back against the seat and her eyes closed. "Can we drive for . . . oh, a thousand miles or so?"

She heard Carson chuckle. "A thousand miles, huh?"

"Yeah. I'll pay for the gas."

He didn't answer and she glanced to her left. He was smiling, looking straight ahead. "I'm glad you're having a nice time," he said.

"Very nice," she replied.

They drove for a while longer. Gracie feared she might fall asleep, but just as soon as she felt herself falling, they slowed and came to a stop.

Jerking upright, she looked to her left. "Are we home?" Immediately, she knew that was a dumb question.

"I thought maybe we'd stop and enjoy the stars," Carson told her. "I hope that's okay."

Gracie leaned back in her seat, looking up at the sky. Carson had pulled off the road into the entrance of an open field. No trees blocked her view. "It's perfect." Suddenly she didn't want to go home. She was tired of being either at the shop or at home.

"You're looking quite relaxed," Carson told her.

Nodding, Gracie closed her eyes. "Ummmm . . . I am."

"So, we made a good decision? Ditching the party and taking a drive, I mean?"

"Ummmm," Gracie agreed. "Excellent decision."

She was sure the wine was making her so relaxed, but it was possible the company and the night air contributed to the effect.

"And stopping here? Is that okay?"

Gracie opened her eyes and looked at Carson. "Yes," she said softly. "It's okay."

He leaned in closer. "I thought you might still be mad at me."

She shook her head. "No. I'm not mad. You were just aggravated at Izzie. I knew that."

She could swear he leaned closer. His lips must be only inches away from hers, she thought. "Where is Izzie, by the way? I haven't seen her the past two days."

"I let her stay in Louisville with Kate, her old babysitter, since there was going to be a lot going on here this week."

He spoke soft and low and Gracie enjoyed watching his lips move. "Oh," she replied.

"So, is it okay if I kiss you?"

The question came out of the blue. Gracie leaned closer and was about to answer when his lips captured hers.

It was a sweet, intoxicating kiss and just the thing to put Gracie over the edge. At the point their lips made contact, she melted, feeling herself pressed against Carson.

His hands gently cupped her face as his lips softly caressed, slowly raking over them in a determined manner. And Gracie was just as determined to give back what she was getting.

So she did.

All too quickly, he pulled away and Gracie discovered she didn't like him not kissing her.

"Well," she said, opening her eyes to look at him. He was still just inches away, looking back into her face. "That was a kiss."

He grinned. "Yes. That was a kiss."

Settling back in her seat, she asked softly, "Why did you kiss me?"

"Because it felt right," he murmured. "And you looked damned kissable."

"Must be the wine," she mumbled. She hadn't felt kissable in some time.

"No, it wasn't the wine," he said, leaning closer again. "It was just you."

Then he did it again.

Gracie felt lost in the feel of his lips on hers. Soft and firm, they moved over hers. She opened hers slightly and his tongue slipped inside her mouth to tango with hers, gentle, easy thrusts mixed with tender kisses. The kiss deepened and Carson moved his hands to her hair, threading his fingers through her tresses as he held her.

Gracie let out a quick breath as his lips left hers and began to trail down her cheek to her neck. She arched her neck, allowing him access as he lowered his kisses toward her collarbone.

She liked him doing that. Way too much.

Nothing she'd ever experienced had felt better. Carson's lips on her neck, planting kisses up and down, made her want to let him devour her. Let him . . .

"Carson," she breathed.

His kisses slowed and she tilted her face back down to look at him. "We should stop," she said.

He studied her face, peering deeply into her eyes. Suddenly, she was afraid of what she saw in his eyes. She didn't want to think about it. Didn't want to know what was going on in that head of his behind his eyes.

"I don't want to do anything that you don't want me to," he said softly.

She nodded, still looking into his eyes. "I need . . . I need to stop, to think."

One corner of his mouth turned up into a grin. "To think?"

"I can't think when you're kissing me like that."

"You're not supposed to," he answered, smiling fully now.

There was something going on with him and Gracie wasn't sure what it was. It scared her.

"Maybe we should head back."

The look on his face scared her even more. She wanted to be here with him, just like this, kissing him. And she didn't. The thing was, she didn't know how to convey that to him She was certain he thought she was giving him the brush-off.

"If you want to, Gracie, then that's what we'll do."

She glanced away, looking out over the field. "I don't know what I want," she whispered, so softly she barely heard it herself. She had no clue whether he heard her.

Turning back to him then, she said, "Yes, I think we should go home now. Please. I hope you understand."

Carson nodded, his facing growing serious. Reaching out, he touched her cheek with the backs of his fingers. "I'm not sure I do," he whispered. "But maybe, in time, I will."

# FOURTEEN

*I don't know what I want.*

Carson had heard the words, barely spoken, as they came from Gracie's lips two nights earlier. She'd avoided him since then and he hadn't pushed the issue. All he could think about, however, was Gracie's lips and how much he had enjoyed kissing them.

She was confused, he thought; and if the truth be known, so was he. He knew why he was confused—he'd vowed not to get involved with anyone until Izzie was older and both their lives were back on track. Until he felt safe again and could trust himself in a relationship with another woman.

Since Marci, he was damned untrusting. He just had no desire to feel again what he'd felt when Marci had left both of them, ripping their lives apart. He never wanted to experience that hopelessness again.

He wished he knew what was going on in Gracie's head. He wished he knew about her past, what had happened with the man whose picture still sat on her bedside table. The one who had died.

Even more, he wanted to know how that man's death affected her life now, for he had a distinct feeling that it did.

The winds picked up outside as rain thrashed against his window. A late-night summer storm had turned brutal. Carson looked out over the street from his living room window and watched the rain come down in slanted sheets while debris was tossed about on the sidewalks. Suddenly, he realized that this might be more than a typical summer thunderstorm. When the emergency warning siren on top of the courthouse down the street went off a few seconds later, his suspicions were confirmed.

About that time a solid upward draft of wind took the awning that hung over his and Gracie's shop doors completely off and tossed it like a wadded-up tissue into the street.

He turned and ran toward his apartment door, shouting Gracie's name.

She met him on the landing outside their apartments, wide-eyed and a sleepy-but-frightened look across her face.

Thunder ripped through the night around them as a flash of lightning split the night. The building moaned under the stress of the windstorm outside; the lights flickered.

"The cellar!" she shouted and grabbed his arm.

He pulled her close, his arms around her, and they both ran down the stairs toward the first-floor landing. Behind the stairwell, Gracie fiddled with another lock, finally opened it, and they began their descent into the dark cellar.

"I can't see," Carson told her.

"Wait." She tugged on his arm.

He heard her fumbling against the wall, and finally a bulb overhead lit the stairway. "There's a flashlight around here somewhere," he heard her say. "There."

Carson looked where she was pointing, fished the flashlight out from between the handrail and the wall, flipped it on, and saw that the batteries were still working. Then he grasped her hand to lead her further into the cellar.

"I haven't been down here in ages," she told him. "I have no clue what's down here."

They'd found the flashlight just in time. With the next flash of lightning, the power went completely out.

Gracie grasped his arm tightly, and he silently and quickly led her away from the side of the cellar with the window wells and underneath the stairway itself. The wind thrashed against the windows and thunder roared above their heads. He flashed the light in the dark corner and found several wooden boxes stacked against the wall underneath the stair.

"Here. Let's get back in here," he told her.

"I don't even want to know what's back there," Gracie told him. He thought she might be hesitant to crawl back under the stairway until a boom and a crash up above sent her into his arms and both of them toppling back against the boxes.

She was shivering in his arms. Carson sat back

against one of the wooden crates and pulled her closer into him. She was practically sitting in his lap, her head against his chest, her arms around him.

And she was wearing that damned sleep shirt he liked so much.

"Are you okay?" he whispered after a minute.

"No."

He smiled to himself. "You're shaking."

"I know."

"I won't let anything happen to you, Gracie."

She nodded against his chest. "I won't let anything happen to you, either."

He smiled again and planted a small kiss on the top of her forehead.

"God, I hate tornadoes," she told him a little later.

"Have you been in many?" he asked.

She shook her head. "Never. But now I know I hate them."

"Maybe it's just a bad thunderstorm. It will be over soon," he promised.

"I'm holding you to that, mister." Carson grinned and held her tighter. Even in the midst of a tornado, she felt so good in his arms and he was very conscious of the fact that that was exactly where he wanted her—in his arms.

Something crashed against the outside wall again; then a tinkling of glass and a whoosh of wind made them aware the storm was still not over. A window well broken behind them, Carson suspected.

They rode out the storm for thirty minutes or longer, and when it finally died down enough that

Carson felt they were safe to move, he told Gracie so.

"Let's wait a little longer," she told him.

"The storm is over, Gracie. Let's go see what kind of damage we have upstairs."

She looked up at him then, her eyes wide. "Oh my! Our shops!"

"Yeah," he answered. "We might want to take a look."

The aftermath of a devastating storm can bring an uncanny silence to its victims as they survey the damages of their surroundings. Carson and Gracie both felt the chilling calm as they moved through their businesses to assess the damages. The power was still out and it was hours until daylight, so they tried to check out what they could by flashlight.

The interior of Gracie's shop had suffered less damage than the storefront. The awning was ripped entirely away, leaving crumbling brick behind. Her flowerpots and window boxes were gone. Totally gone. A bench, which at one time sat to the right of her door, had been thrust into the building and was now reduced to nothing more than potential toothpick material. It had narrowly missed her window, and Gracie was thankful for that. Inside, water had been forced under the front door and around the window, but all that was ruined were some Oriental rugs on the floor.

Carson's side, however, hadn't fare quite so well.

When the awning was ripped from the building, a metal support pole thrust through the window had shattered it. Glass was blown inward and scattered about the room, along with a vast amount of water. Everything in the room was water-soaked. Arcade games were blown over; everything behind the bar— liquor bottles and glasses—was scattered and broken, the wide-screened television was ruined. The force of the winds must have been enormously strong, Carson thought to himself, in order to do this much damage inside the building.

They surveyed the aftermath wordlessly. Finally, Carson turned to Gracie, a sick, sinking feeling in the pit of his stomach. "I'm going to see if I can find some plywood to board up that window. That's about all we can do tonight without power. We're going to have our work cut out for us tomorrow."

Gracie nodded and slowly panned the room. "I'm just glad Izzie wasn't here," she said quietly.

Carson had thought of that earlier. "Yes. I know."

Gracie looked at him then with a terrified expression on her face. "Carson," she began hesitantly, 'we're often in the same storm path as Louisville. Maybe you should call."

At that instant the sinking feeling in his gut turned to dread. "You're right."

Within the next several minutes, Carson had called Kate on his cell phone and found out that the storm had skirted Louisville. Izzie had slept through the entire thing. But Kate had heard the news reports and was relieved to find out that everyone was okay in Franklinville. He made arrangements with Kate for Izzie to stay another couple of days while they cleaned up the shops, then boarded up the front window while Gracie headed back upstairs to check out the condition of both apartments.

It was in her bedroom that Carson found her several minutes later, lying curled on her side in her bed, softly crying into her pillow.

He didn't know anything else to do but to go to her. Lying down beside her, he pulled Gracie into his arms and she turned into him, wrapping her arms about his waist and snuggling close. Her head was tucked beneath his chin and his fingers went to her cheek to gently stroke her hair away.

She sobbed softly and he just held her. He supposed all of this was just a lot to absorb.

"Shshsh . . ." he cooed. "Everything is all right now."

She didn't answer, but clung to him, sniffling.

Carson didn't know when a woman had ever felt so good in his arms. The past two nights he'd dreamed of holding her and tenderly making love to her. It was something he'd decided, if given the chance, he had to risk—not just making love with her, but *loving* her. He'd decided that loving Gracie was worth the risk, even if it turned out to be painful for him in the end. Making love with her would simply be the icing on the cake.

Loving her mind and soul and heart were first and foremost in his mind. Loving her body was secondary. But oh, what pleasure he imagined that would bring.

And yes, it was worth risking the pain to know the pleasure of loving Gracie.

"Tell me why you're so upset," he whispered to

her. The room was dark except for the dull glow of an emergency-powered street lamp outside her window. Carson kept his eyes closed and gently caressed her cheek, seeing her beautiful face with his mind's eye.

"It's just—" she whispered and then paused. "It just hit me, we could have lost everything."

"But we didn't."

"I'm glad Izzie wasn't here," she said again.

"Me, too."

She fell silent, still sniffling once in a while. He just held her closer.

"I lost everything in my life once," she said after another few minutes. "I don't want that to ever happen to me again."

Carson thought about that. "When Marci left, I thought my world was going to end," he told her. "But at least I still had Izzie and my job. I survived. I'm not sure what it would feel like to lose everything."

Gracie took a deep breath and slowly exhaled. "It's hell," she whispered.

Carson decided to take a risk. "Tell me about it, Gracie."

For a while all he heard, all he felt, was her breathing. She took in long, even breaths and let them slowly out against his chest. After a few minutes, she pulled away and looked into his face. They both lay there, heads facing each other on the pillow.

"All I ever wanted to do with my life was to dance," she began softly. "It was all I ever did as a child, and my parents helped me reach that dream by sending me to the finest dance instructors. When I graduated from high school, I went to New York. In no time I was dancing with a very prestigious troupe and was making quite a name for myself. I was living my dream and every minute of my existence was focused on that dream. I was consumed for several years. And then I met Evan."

She stopped and Carson said nothing. All he wanted to do was listen.

"Evan wasn't a dancer and it was a fluke that we even met because all my time was spent on the road or practicing. We bumped into each other on the subway one afternoon and it was a magical, love-at-first-sight kind of thing."

Carson couldn't tell, but he thought he saw a glimmer in her eye as she talked about him. He wondered if that glimmer were a tear or a twinkle from a fond memory.

"He was a stockbroker, knew nothing about the dance world, but he loved me. And I loved him. We were planning to be married, the date was set. Then . . ."

She closed her eyes and Carson felt her tense. Reaching over, he stroked her cheek again and caught a tear that had escaped from beneath an eyelid. Tears. What he'd seen were still tears. He was moved by her sadness and only wanted to protect her more, to ease her pain, for he could feel her pain as well.

"You don't have to go on if you don't want to," he whispered. He didn't want her to endure this for his sake, but he had a feeling she needed to continue.

She shook her head. "I want to," she murmured.

He let her gather herself again, waiting. After a couple of minutes, she resumed her story.

"We both had a weekend off and had decided to take a drive out of the city, just to get away from the rat race for a while. We had no plans, were just out for a leisurely Saturday afternoon in the country. Our excursion didn't last long. It started raining and Evan lost control of his car on a curve when a large truck met us nearly head on. We skidded into the guardrail and flipped over a hill.

"Evan died immediately. I was conscious and lay there until help arrived. It was horrible and seemed like hours. I knew he was dead. My right leg was badly broken and I had a few other cuts and bruises, but I was alive.

"Unfortunately, I wasn't able to dance again."

"Why?"

"The leg took months to heal. It was a difficult break in two places. My life was in such a dark cloud, I didn't care about doing physical therapy or even trying to dance again. I would have traded my dancing career for Evan's life, but that was impossible. So, I decided that dancing would never be a part of my life again and I just didn't do what I needed to do to get the leg back in shape. It just wasn't in me. I couldn't.

"After a while, I came back to Franklinville. My father had died a year before the accident. My mother had died a couple of years prior to that.

This building was my father's and part of my inheritance. It took me a while, but I eventually turned to something other than dancing. That's when Romantically Yours was born. And ever since then, this is all I have had. All I've wanted. Until . . ."

She didn't finish her thought. Carson wanted badly to know where that thought was leading, but he was sure she wasn't going to say anymore. He wanted to draw her closer, to hold her next to his heart and keep her there, but he was afraid she'd pull back, that this wasn't the time. So, he simply watched her.

"Has there been no one in your life since then?"

Gracie looked intently into his eyes. "No," she whispered. "It's just too damned scary."

He searched her face. It was now or never, and he didn't know if there would ever be another opportunity like this one. He had to tell her, in some subtle way, how he felt about her. That he loved her. But he didn't want to frighten her away.

That's what scared the hell out of him.

"What if there were someone else who was scared, too?" he asked softly, his fingertips stroking her chin and lips. "What if that someone were willing to risk falling in love again, even though he was scared to death, too? What if, for him, it were worth the risk? Would you still be scared?"

The tears that fell down Gracie's cheeks were fat and big and the sob that choked from her throat tore at Carson's heart. "I would still be scared," she said, barely louder than a breath, her gaze clinging to his. "But not as much if I knew we could be scared together."

It was as though his heart burst then, with all the love and tenderness he wanted to show to Gracie pouring forth. He kissed her, and her lips tasted like a fine wine. Within seconds, he was drunk with the thought of loving her for the rest of his life and he kissed her again.

Gracie knew nothing else but to finally let go.

The touch of Carson's lips to hers allowed her the surrender for which she'd ached for years. It was like a huge release, an enormous burden that had been lifted from her shoulders and out of her mind, melting away with a whoosh as his hands drew tenderly over her face and his lips softly caressed hers. He whispered her name, over and over, and Gracie never wanted him to stop.

She'd denied for so long that she possessed incredibly deep feelings for Carson. She'd denied that she could be in love with him. But this moment—this precise moment in time—was the one she'd remember for her lifetime as the one where she'd finally let it all go.

All of it. The past. Her ache for a future with a husband and a child. Her fear of falling in love again. Her fear of having that love snatched away.

She could finally let it go. She could finally risk loving again. And she wanted to love Carson.

There was nothing to do but experience the emotion that washed over the two of them. There was nothing to do but to feel. No thinking, the thinking had all been done. What remained for the two of them was to experience each other and to explore their passion and their love.

Carson's hand slipped underneath Gracie's night-shirt and she shivered as his fingers slid up her thigh and over her hip. Raw tingles of passion snaked through her as those same fingers gently teased their way up her waist to the tender area just beneath one breast. He gently cupped her and Gracie moaned and moved closer into his hand while he caressed and thumbed her nipple.

His mouth still consumed hers, their tongues slowly mingling and parrying with each other. Gracie let Carson take the lead, weary of being the strong independent woman she'd been for the past ten years, just wanting to absorb his attention and his ministrations and revel in the passionate flames he was stoking inside her.

For the first time in a long time, she just wanted to feel thoroughly loved.

Her nightshirt was gone within seconds; Carson slowly slipped it over her head and rolled her onto her back. He covered her body with his and gazed into her eyes while he made lazy circles with his fingertips at her temples. Gracie reached up and touched her tongue to his lips.

Once. Twice. Then again.

The fourth time she teased him with her tongue, Carson grasped her face with his hands and held her to him as he devoured her lips with his mouth, then rained kisses all over her face.

"Gracie," he breathed, "I want you to be sure. I don't want to do anything that you're not ready to—"

"Make love to me, Carson," she breathed back between his kisses. "I want you to make love to me."

He answered her desire with a groan and the quick removal of his clothing. Gracie knew that there was no turning back now, that once she'd succumbed to Carson's passion, she would have difficulty separating herself emotionally from him should there ever come a time that she would be forced to do that.

But she was willing to take the risk.

His warm body felt so wonderful over hers as he covered her again, one of his legs nudging gently between her thighs. The next seconds, minutes, hours were simply filled with sensation and kisses and touches as Carson explored her body from the tip of her nose to the valley between her breasts and traveling further to rain kisses on her belly and lower.

He lingered between her thighs, bringing sweet ecstasy to her as his lips nibbled and played and his tongue made love to her. And when Gracie could take no more of this pleasure, she reached for him, wanting him inside her, urging his body up and over hers.

He kissed her then with unbridled passion, and within seconds, Gracie felt him nudge her thighs further apart and slip himself inside her body.

The length of him filled her and Gracie exhaled deeply at the fulfillment she felt and at the sudden serenity that overtook her soul. But she didn't have long to revel in that completeness for passion overtook both of them in a frenzied whirl as the night consumed them and surrounded them with pleasures they'd both long forgotten and possibly had never experienced before.

Some time later, Gracie lay peacefully content by Carson's side, her heart and body and soul full of him, feeling totally and completely in love.

And she wasn't frightened. Not at all.

They slept, and when they woke early the next morning, they loved each other all over again.


The next two days were total, unadulterated bliss.

Carson and Gracie took turns working and cleaning up each other's shops and sleeping in each other's beds. They rested often, taking frequent naps throughout the day, justifying to each other that the after-storm cleanup was zapping a lot of their energy and that they needed frequent naps to keep up their strength.

The thing was, their nap times nearly always turned into lovemaking time, with both being left more exhausted after their naps than before.

But they didn't care. They were in love. And everything else paled in comparison.

By Saturday afternoon they were ready to fetch Izzie from Louisville and Gracie went with Carson to get her. Izzie didn't say anything for a long time, but just kept looking strangely at the two of them while they had dinner in Louisville, when they stopped for ice cream on the way home, and then later as they watched a movie in Carson's apartment.

"So, are you guys in love or something?" she finally blurted out, turning to her father.

Carson was surprised at the child's question. He and Gracie had decided that they weren't going to say anything to Izzie yet, but let things progress naturally. They'd avoided too much contact, not even holding hands, thinking that she wouldn't notice anything.

Obviously, Izzie was more in tune with them than either had expected.

Carson glanced to Gracie, who had blushed at Izzie's question.

"You know Gracie and I are friends, Izzie."

The child passed her gaze back and forth between the two. "Hmmmm . . ." she said. "Friends."

She didn't say anything else the remainder of the evening until Carson tucked her into bed a couple of hours later. "You can't trick me, Dad," she told her father. "I know there is something going on with you two."

Carson just smiled and pinched her cheek and bid her good night without another word. A part of him wanted to share how he felt about Gracie with his daughter. Another part of him, the protecting part, wanted to wait. That was the nagging part that told him to be cautious, to make sure before involving Izzie too deeply.

But all in all, life was good; and after Izzie was fast asleep, he made love to Gracie in her bed before slipping back into his own in the wee hours.

Then on Sunday morning, he woke to a phone call that abruptly sent his world into an out-of-control downward spiral.

# FIFTEEN

"Guess who's here!"

Izzie raced in the back door of Romantically Yours Sunday afternoon, Bandit nipping at her heels. Claire, sleeping at Gracie's feet, barely raised an eyelid at the pup. Gracie glanced up from her computer where she was attempting to determine the cost to replace the Oriental rugs and the awning that were damaged in the storm. She was so used to Izzie breezing in and out that she barely glanced up as she searched her inventory list.

"Who?"

"My mother!"

"That's nice." Gracie's gaze trailed the list. Perhaps it's in another file, she thought.

"And she is so cool! She's got long black hair and a small tattoo on her shoulder and she brought some movie pictures for me to look at and a new baseball bat—I'm so glad she's finally realized that I don't like dolls—and her lips are really red and her teeth are really white and she is so-o-o-o beautiful and she's staying for three whole days, maybe longer!"

"Uh-huh."

"And she and my dad look so-o-o-o-o perfect together."

At that statement Gracie finally looked up. A twinge of something she couldn't readily describe settled deep in her belly. Something that made her a bit queasy. Something telling her that things weren't quite . . . right.

*Who looked perfect together?*

She looked Izzie square in the eyes. "Who did you say is here?"

"My mother!"

"Your mother." The words barely escaped her lips. Gracie sank back in her chair and stared at the girl. Marci was here?

"I bet you're excited, huh?" The words fumbled off her tongue. Try as she might, she couldn't let Izzie know that she was upset by her news.

"She is so beautiful, Gracie. And I love her so much. I hope she stays longer than three days."

Gracie swallowed. "And where . . . where is she staying?"

"With us!" The child jumped up in excitement. "Well, I just had to tell you. I have to get back to my dad and mom! I'm so excited! We're a family again!"

*Her dad and mom. Family.*

Izzie, as was her style, was gone in a flash. Gracie sank lower into her chair, feeling like a deflated balloon.

She didn't know what to do, so she did nothing.

For the remainder of the afternoon, she stayed in the shop. Later, she holed herself up in her apartment. This was none of her business; she'd just have to wait for Carson to make an explanation. For him to tell her that Izzie had blown things all out of proportion, that she'd misunderstood. That Marci was just passing through town and would be gone within the hour. She was sure he would do that . . . soon.

Any minute, probably.

Thing was, he didn't.

It was Monday afternoon before she saw him, and that was only briefly as he and Izzie and Marci got into his ex-wife's car and drove away. It was late Monday evening when she finally talked to him, although he only spoke a brief hello as he ushered his "family" up the back stairs and into his apartment. His gaze had lingered on her but Gracie had glanced away too quickly to try and read his eyes. She was so confused, didn't know what to think. She longed for an explanation from him, but she obviously wasn't going to get one. She couldn't help, though, but take in the radiant gleam of happiness on Izzie's face and the attractiveness of her mother. Izzie was definitely right when she'd said her mother was beautiful.

But the thing that bothered her most was the fact that Marci's little black rental sedan had sat parked all Sunday night out back beside Carson's Corvette. It hadn't budged until the entire family took it out Monday afternoon.

And apparently, neither had Marci. Both were still there late Monday evening.

Gracie thought about the entire situation for hours that night. By Tuesday morning, she'd made her decision.

By noon, she'd left Franklinville.


Izzie was ecstatic.

Carson was miserable.

And if she'd be honest with herself and admit it, Carson knew Marci was miserable as well.

As he stared across his living room at mother and daughter curled up on the couch together watching television, he couldn't help but wonder why he'd not seen through Marci years earlier. Izzie was chattering away, informing her mother of the antics of her favorite cartoon characters. Marci listened intently, asking this question and that, laughing and smiling.

Acting all the while.

Marci was definitely in her element. She'd been an actress since birth. She was no more comfortable with the "mom" scenario than he'd be on a stage.

He just hoped sooner or later his daughter would see though Marci's performance.

Suddenly, he missed Gracie like crazy. He so much enjoyed the genuine laughter she and his daughter shared. He loved the way Gracie ruffled Izzie's bangs and crouched down to get on her level when she talked to her. He adored the fact that Gracie adored his daughter.

He missed her. And it was high time he told her what was going on. He should have before this.

Rising, he told the pair on the couch that he needed to go downstairs for a few minutes. Instead, he slipped into the hallway and gently rapped on Gracie's door. After a while and no answer, he realized it was Tuesday and that she'd be at the shop.

But the back shop door was locked. The front door as well. The thing that sent shivers of dread deep into his gut was the sign on the front door that read "Closed Indefinitely."

It was then he knew he'd screwed up. Royally.

On Thursday morning Carson walked into Amie's Place loaded for bear. He'd had just about enough of Amie and Constance and all the others directly avoiding his queries about where Gracie had gone, and he was out for some answers.

Now.

How his life had suddenly gone haywire, he had no clue. Of course, it all had to do with Marci. Just one more thing for which he could never forgive her.

But he wasn't going to think of that now. No time. His prime concern at the moment was Gracie, where in the hell she was, the reason she'd left, and to what conclusions she must have jumped before she had.

If he could only talk to her. If she'd only waited until he could explain the situation and discuss what was happening. She'd misunderstood, he was sure.

Dammit! He should have spoken to her Monday afternoon when they'd passed on the stairs. It was just so damned awkward, he hadn't been able to.

He'd avoided Gracie the past couple of days but had thought she would have realized that Izzie needed to spend time with her mother. He hadn't intended for that time to always include the three of them, but that was the way Izzie wanted it. He guessed the child needed that sense of family. Even if it were only brief. That was the one thing he wanted to tell Gracie. That was the reason he'd come to her shop Tuesday afternoon when he'd found her gone. He just wanted to tell her he was doing it for Izzie's sake. That nothing had changed between the two of them.

"Honey bun?"

Carson whipped his attention to the young girl behind the counter. He hadn't realized she was standing there looking at him until this moment.

"Uh . . . no," he answered. "Is Amie around? I need to talk to her."

"I'm right here."

The voice came from his left. Turning, he looked at Gracie's friend. Her face was stern, her mouth in a frown. I'm not in the mood for a runaround, he thought to himself. Please just answer my questions.

"Let's sit over here." She motioned to a table next to the window. He followed and the girl behind the counter brought them both coffee.

Carson didn't think he'd be there long enough for it to cool off, but he took it anyway.

He sat across from Amie and looked directly into

her eyes. "Please tell me where Gracie has gone," he pleaded softly with her.

Amie closed her eyes and took in a breath. When she opened them, Carson knew he wasn't going to get the answers he sought. "I don't know where she is, Carson. She only left a message on my answering machine at home saying she would be back later in the week."

Later in the week. Maybe that would be today, he thought.

"Did she say why she left?"

Amie shook her head.

He glanced away.

"I have to talk to her, Amie. If I could just call her, explain something—"

"I think explaining would probably be in order. In fact, perhaps you should have done that a little sooner."

Ah. So Amie did know more than she was letting on.

He looked at her again. "It was a difficult situation."

"Gracie is an understanding woman."

"I know that."

"You should have trusted her to understand."

"I know that, too."

"You shouldn't have avoided her."

"It wasn't that, Amie. There was more to it than that. It was Izzie; she was just so—"

He didn't go on. There was no need for him to hash this out with Amie. Standing, he tossed a dollar bill onto the table for his coffee. "If you see her, just tell her I need to talk to her. If she calls, tell her, too. Will you please do that for me?"

Amie's face softened and she nodded. "Yes. I'll do that, Carson. I'll tell her."

With a jerk of his head, he told her, "Thanks," then left the restaurant. A fear like he'd never known gripped him like a knife to the gut. He'd lost her. And then he reminded himself that he'd consciously decided to take the risk to love her, and that Gracie was worth the pain.

Every minute he'd loved her was worth it.

He just hadn't known it would hurt this bad.

It was late Saturday evening when Gracie came home. With her heart guarded and her mind made up, she quietly made her way up the back stairway to her apartment, careful not to wake her next-door neighbors. There was one thing she noted as she'd pulled into her parking space behind the shops— Marci's car was gone. She didn't know what that meant, but it didn't alter her plans. Not one bit.

It didn't matter to her anymore whether Marci meant anything at all to Carson, or even whether she slept in his bed. All that mattered was that Gracie knew that *she* was the only person she could ever depend on. All Gracie Hart would ever have was herself, and it was high time she accepted that fact.

She would remain firm in her convictions and she would not be swayed. She'd found the solitude she longed for in her stay in the mountains the past few days. The pain was still there, would always be there.

She'd learned to live with it before; she'd learn to live with it again.

The thing she knew more than anything else, however, was that she would never risk the pain again.

There would be no children, no husbands, no lovers in her life. That just appeared to be her destiny. There would be no more Romantically Yours, either.

She'd found a new place to start over, and that's what she intended to do.

New shop. New friends. New life.

She'd done it before; she'd do it again.

There was only one task remaining. One more thing she had to take care of. And she would do that first thing in the morning. There was no use dragging this out.

It was time to get on with her life. Without Carson and Izzie.

# SIXTEEN

Carson woke with thoughts of Gracie running through his head. Every morning this week, he'd done that. He couldn't rid his mind or his heart of her. He wanted her to come back so badly he ached inside.

And poor Izzie. She'd been through it, too. What a topsy-turvy emotional week for the two of them. He hoped he'd never have to go through anything like that ever again.

He needed Gracie and so did Izzie. They both loved her.

There was nothing he could do, however, until she returned; so he set about to making things as normal as possible for his daughter.

He rose from his bed and went straight to the coffeemaker. It was still early and Izzie probably wouldn't be up for a while yet, so he decided to walk to the newsstand on the corner to pick up a Sunday paper before he fixed pancakes for their breakfast. A leisurely few minutes drinking coffee and reading the paper would be just the right start for his day.

As soon as he stepped through the back door, however, he realized that a leisurely cup of coffee and the morning paper would be out of the question.

Gracie was back. Her Miata was parked behind the shop. He wasted no time in turning back into the building and heading up the stairway to her apartment.

Gracie was about to open her door when she heard the knock. She didn't give herself time to prepare for who might be on the other side, she simply opened the door and waited.

It was Carson.

Somehow she'd known it would be.

"I was just getting ready to come see you," she said, her voice controlled and her demeanor businesslike. It was the only way she could get through this, she'd decided: To act as if nothing had ever happened between them and end everything before it got out of hand.

"I was just coming to see you." Carson smiled, and it was extremely difficult for Gracie not to smile back and jump into his arms. But she would stand firm. She had to.

"Come in, then." She opened the door and stepped aside as Carson brushed by her. He made his way to the sofa and sat. Gracie chose an armchair to his left.

A moment of awkwardness swept by them, then Gracie said, "I've made a decision while I was away the past few days. I'm selling the building. I'm giving you first shot at buying me out."

She could tell from the look on Carson's face that her statement had come from way out in left field. There was nothing more she wanted to say, so she waited for him to respond. His response was not at all what she expected.

"We need to talk, Gracie. And not about you selling this building. We need to talk about us."

"There is no *us.*"

The pain that raced across his face was almost more than she could bear. Gracie glanced away.

"A week ago, there was an *us.* We need to talk about that. About what happened."

Gracie shook her head, still not looking at him.

"Talk to me Gracie. Let me know what you're thinking."

She turned to him them. "You're a fine one to tell me to talk. You avoided me for two entire days. I think you should have taken that initiative a few days earlier."

She could tell she'd hit a nerve and she was almost sorry she'd said what she had, but she needed to be done with him.

He nodded slowly. "You're right. So, I'll talk to you now."

"It's too late. I don't want to hear it."

"Well, you're going to hear it, whether you want to or not."

Gracie stood and walked to the fireplace, her back

to Carson and her arms crossed over her chest. "I'm moving in a month. I've already found a place. I'll be putting the building on the market next week unless you want to make me a deal. That's all I want to talk about."

There was silence behind her. A long, thorough silence. For a moment, she thought he might have left the room. Finally, she turned to see him staring into the floor, his elbows propped on his knees, his head in his hands.

When she turned to him, he looked up, too.

"Gracie," he said softly, "we have to talk about what happened this week. We have to. Please, let me explain."

She felt her shoulders slump and fought hard to keep her resolve, but she supposed she needed to hear what he had to say.

"So tell me," she whispered.

"Please come here. I can't talk to you when you're standing way over there." He reached out his hand but Gracie could only stare at it. She wanted to take it but was afraid that with one touch, the shield she'd built around her heart would crumble and she'd fall into him and give it all up.

She couldn't do that.

"I'll sit over here." She moved to the chair again, dismissing his hand. Carson dropped it and watched her until she was settled. "So, tell me what you need to tell me," she said, "but nothing you say is going to change my mind."

Carson took a deep breath and peered into her eyes. It was all Gracie could do to keep her gaze connected with his; she wanted so much to glance away. "Marci was here for Izzie, Gracie, not me. I did it for my daughter. She wanted so badly to spend time with her mother."

"You could have told me that," she bit back quickly. It wasn't that she hadn't known that already; it was that he'd not approached her with this knowledge. She knew how badly Izzie needed to see her mother.

"There wasn't an opportunity. It all took me by surprise so damned quickly. I wasn't prepared for Izzie's reaction to Marci. I just couldn't break the child's heart . . ."

Gracie empathized with him. He'd been in a difficult situation. She also knew that it would continue to be a difficult situation for a long, long time.

"Izzie needed her mother. I know that," she confirmed.

"Then why did you leave? Why did you go without a word to me? Gracie, I've been crazy for the past few days worrying about you."

His eyes pleaded with her. Gracie couldn't look at them any longer. After a moment of staring off into the room, she turned back to him. "According to Izzie, you and Marci are perfect together. Perhaps that's a child's perspective and irrational, I don't know, but it's entirely possible that she's right. The three of you looked like a family the other day. Izzie was beaming. It was apparent she was happy. I've never see her that happy.

"Carson, I decided to bow out for a few days. I decided that perhaps you and Izzie and Marci needed that time. It wasn't a heroic act or anything special on my part; it was just what I felt needed to be done. Marci was obviously there and Izzie needed her. I didn't need to be in the picture."

"I needed you," he returned softly, but he didn't let her linger on that statement for long. "You're right, though. Izzie did need and want Marci. But I didn't. I was miserable and uncomfortable."

"She stayed in your apartment." She tried not to make it sound like an accusation, but was afraid she didn't pull it off.

He nodded. "Yes, she stayed Sunday night. Izzie insisted, wouldn't let her leave. She slept in Izzie's bed with her. I couldn't deny either of them that. Please don't hold that against me. It was what I thought was right at the time. She didn't stay any longer than that night. I insisted she get a motel room after that."

Gracie closed her eyes, wondering how she could have let things get so blown out of proportion. She knew Carson loved Izzie and would do anything for her. She also knew of Izzie's infatuation with her mother.

But the fact remained that she'd made up her mind. None of that made a difference anymore. She was leaving and that was all there was to it.

"Marci left Thursday for California," Carson said then. Gracie glanced sharply up at his words. "She didn't say goodbye. She left a note on the door sometime in the night. Izzie had some crazy notion we were going to California with her. That we were all going to be a family. She thought we were getting married again. I told her those things were never going to happen.

"She's devastated. Her heart is broken. Friday was a long day. Yesterday she was better. I'm hoping by today she will have forgotten most of it."

Gracie's heart was breaking for Izzie. It was the first thing she'd allowed herself to feel in days and it was damned hard for her to keep her emotions in check. "I'm sorry Izzie's having a hard time. I wish I could—"

"I love you, Gracie. I want you to spend the rest of your life with me. With Izzie and me."

She couldn't sit there any longer. Abruptly, she stood and stepped back toward the mantel again. She couldn't look at Carson. Couldn't. She might just blow everything.

He loved her.

She couldn't handle that. Not now.

"Spend the day with us. Just the day. Please do that for me."

Gracie turned and looked into Carson's face and almost told him she would. Something inside her wanted her to say *yes,* another part of her was telling her to hold back with all her strength.

She shook her head no. "I don't think that's a good idea, Carson. I don't think we should spend any more time together. Izzie has been through enough heartache this week. I'm leaving soon; I don't want to add to her heartache."

Carson looked deep into her eyes and then stood. "Well, you're certainly adding to mine," he said quietly. He stood for several minutes, watching her, as if he expected her to say something. Finally, he stepped closer. "It's a shame that you can't face this head-on. You're running again, you know, just as you did before. When you lost Evan and your dance career, you didn't fight to get anything back; you ran away from it and for years you were afraid to try again. Now that you've tried, suddenly you're afraid of what that might mean and you're running again.

"Don't Gracie. Don't give in to it. Sure, life dealt you a bad hand years ago. Don't let it deal you another. This time you have the power to make things turn out differently.

"I'm alive and so is Izzie. We love you. And we're not going anywhere. You're the one who has the power to make it work. All you have to do is stick around. Be the first person in our lives to do that for us, okay? Be the first person in our lives to stay."

In the next instant, he left her alone. And Gracie suddenly realized she didn't like being alone anymore.

Carson let her be after that. Gracie didn't open the shop. Instead, she cleaned closets and packed some things and canceled orders and prepared for a final close-out sale scheduled for the end of the month.

There was no turning back. She was leaving.

She avoided Izzie as much as possible, hoping to make it easier on the child. Izzie didn't understand, but Gracie felt that in the end it would be easier this way.

Amie tried to talk her out of leaving.

Constance and her cronies attempted every trick in the book to get her to admit that she was in love with Carson. It didn't work. None of it worked. She was glad when they finally left her alone.

Still, his words nagged at her. She knew he was right. She was running. Running fast and hard away from him. From love.

From life.

Just as she'd done all those years ago.

Thing was, the ball was rolling now and she didn't know how to stop it. Even if she wanted, she wasn't sure if she could.

It was Wednesday afternoon when a small knock sounded on her apartment door and Gracie answered it. Izzie stood with a scowl on her face on the other side.

"Can I come in?" the child asked.

"*May* I?" Gracie corrected.

"I may?"

Gracie hesitated, smiled at her comeback, then let her. She'd avoided this all week.

Izzie stomped to the sofa and sat down, her arms crossed over her chest. "I'm mad," she announced.

Puzzled, Gracie crossed the room and sat beside her on the sofa. "Do you want to tell me about it?"

"Sure do," she proclaimed. "I'm mad at you."

Gracie tried not to smile; Izzie's face was screwed up into an awful expression. Why are you mad at me, Izzie?"

" 'Cause you been 'noring us."

" 'Noring you?"

"Yes."

"I have?"

"Yes."

"And you don't like that?"

"No. And neither does my dad."

"Oh."

"He's been awful grouchy this week. That's why I'm mad at you."

"I'm sorry, Iz. I've just been busy."

"And you left us last week. Where did you go?" Izzie turned her face up to Gracie's then and her scowl suddenly turned to one of question.

"I . . ." Gracie wasn't quite sure what to say. "I had some business to take care of."

"You didn't see my mom."

"Yes. I saw her."

"You didn't meet her though."

"No. I guess I didn't."

Izzie shook her head. "She didn't like us much. She left us again. I don't think my dad was happy when she was here. I don't think my mom liked visiting us. I think I've decided that she should stay in California."

It was a mouthful, and at the same time, Izzie's words were full of so much meaning. Gracie wondered if Izzie really understood the significance of her own words. Thing was, Gracie understood it completely.

"Well, I gotta go now."

Gracie smiled. "But you just got here."

"I know. Got things to do."

"Will you come back?"

"Maybe."

"Well, bye then."

"Bye!"

And then she was gone again.

Gracie contemplated her visitor for the next few hours. She ate a salad for dinner and had just settled in to read awhile before bed, when another knock sounded at her door.

Again, Izzie stood at her threshold with Bandit tucked under one arm and a small package in her hand.

"I got something for you," she told Gracie.

Thrusting the package forward, Izzie cocked her head to one side. "From me and my dad."

Gracie crouched down on Izzie's level and opened the package. Inside, she found two red construction paper hearts. In a childish scrawl was Carson's name was on one; Izzie's on the other. Gracie took them out of the box and looked at Izzie.

"Turn them over," Izzie said.

Gracie did. "We miss you," was written in white crayon on the first one. "We love you," was written on the second.

Gracie looked back at Izzie, trying to ignore the mist of tears that was glazing her eyes. "Did you make these?"

Izzie shrugged. "Yeah. It was all the paper we had at home. I guess maybe we could have bought a pretty card like what's in your shop downstairs."

Grinning, Gracie reached out and touched Izzie's cheek. "No," she whispered. "These are perfect."

Her eyes were beginning to spill over now and something funny was happening with her heart.

"There's more," Izzie told her then, not giving Gracie much time to think about her gift of two hearts.

She reached into her pocket and pulled out another box, a smaller one, then thrust it to Gracie, too. Bandit struggled in her arm; she let the pup down on the floor. Claire sauntered out the door and the pup chased her down the stairs with a yip and a high-pitched growl.

Suddenly, things seemed back to normal.

Hesitantly, she reached for the box and slowly untied the ribbon. "I can't imagine what this is," she said softly.

"It's better than our two hearts," Izzie proclaimed.

Gracie didn't think anything would be better than getting their two hearts for a gift.

As she lifted the lid on the box, she barely noticed the shadow moving up behind Izzie until Carson crouched down beside the child. She looked at him just as the lid flipped back and the diamond ring sitting inside shone back at her.

"It's a ring," Izzie announced. "Better than our dumb hearts, huh?"

Gracie looked into Carson's eyes. "Your hearts aren't dumb, Izzie. I love both your hearts."

Carson grinned, and she saw the relief wash over his face, followed by an expression of pure love. After a moment, Gracie allowed herself to grin, too.

"My dad wants you to marry us," Izzie said. "That's why he gave you the ring." She crowded in between the two adults and sat on Carson's knee. Gracie was still having a hard time taking her eyes off Carson's face. She loved him so, and for the first time, she wasn't afraid to admit it.

"So, will you just marry us?" Izzie questioned impatiently.

"Yes. Marry us," Carson whispered. "Please don't leave us. Marry us."

"Dad says if you marry us, we will be a family."

Gracie looked at Izzie. How she loved that child, too. "Yes, I suppose we would."

"He says that maybe even someday, we could have a little sister or brother for me. That is, of course, if you decide to marry us."

It was at that moment Gracie knew her resolve had melted and was about to stream down her face. Through a veil of tears, she looked at Carson. "Izzie, what else does your daddy say?"

But Izzie didn't answer, Carson did when he leaned forward and captured her lips with his for a sweet and heartfelt kiss. "He says, he wants you to marry us quickly so we can get started on that baby brother or sister real soon," he whispered into her ear. "Please don't leave us, Gracie. I love you. Izzie loves you. We need you in our lives."

Gracie pulled away and looked at both Izzie and Carson. "How could I leave," she finally said, looking down at the gifts in her hands, "when I'm holding your two hearts in my hand?"

Izzie fell off Carson's knee when he leaned forward to take Gracie in his arms, then kissed her thoroughly one more time.

"You didn't say yes," he told her between kisses.

"Yes. Yes, I'll stay. I'll marry you," Gracie replied, kissing him back. "I'll marry the both of you."

Izzie crowded closer, her arms around the two of them. "Oooh, yuck," she interjected. "Lovey-dovey stuff."

"Get used to it, Munchkin," Carson told his daughter between nibbles of Gracie's lips. "Get used to it."

Izzie kissed them both on the cheek and drew back, looking longingly into Gracie's apartment. "If you guys are gonna do this yucky kissy stuff, mind if I take a bubble bath in your tub, Gracie? Will you bring me the fake champagne in a minute?"

Laughing, Gracie told her to go for it. In a whirlwind, Izzie raced through her apartment, dropping articles of clothing all the way.

"Take all the time you want, Izzie," Gracie called out after her.

"My name is Isabella!"

"I think my tomboy is gone," Carson told her, grinning.

Gracie shrugged. "Naw. She'll always be there, deep down inside."

"I think I'm gonna miss her."

"No, you won't, not for long. I have plans for you, mister, and it has something to do with this incessant ticking clock in my head. I need you to silence it. Immediately."

Gracie smiled at the puzzled expression on Carson's face. She'd tell him about it all later. Much later. When Izzie was tucked into bed for the night and she and Carson could have the bubble bath all to themselves.

Let it not be said that the local diva of romance didn't know how to properly seduce the future father of her child.

## *ABOUT THE AUTHOR*

Maddie James, aka Kim Whalen, grew up in the small farming community of New Holland, Ohio, where her parents still reside. A graduate of Morehead State University and the University of Kentucky, she now lives in central Kentucky with her two teenagers while juggling both a writing career and a career in education. As the early childhood education director for her school system, she's continually amazed by the wisdom of preschoolers. She hopes to bring some of that wit and wisdom to the children in her stories. You can write to her at MJames5359@aol.com.

# BOOK YOUR PLACE ON OUR WEBSITE AND MAKE THE READING CONNECTION!

We've created a customized website just for our very special readers, where you can get the inside scoop on everything that's going on with Zebra, Pinnacle and Kensington books.

When you come online, you'll have the exciting opportunity to:

- View covers of upcoming books
- Read sample chapters
- Learn about our future publishing schedule (listed by publication month *and author*)
- Find out when your favorite authors will be visiting a city near you
- Search for and order backlist books from our online catalog
- Check out author bios and background information
- Send e-mail to your favorite authors
- Meet the Kensington staff online
- Join us in weekly chats with authors, readers and other guests
- Get writing guidelines
- AND MUCH MORE!

**Visit our website at
http://www.zebrabooks.com**

# Put a Little Romance in Your Life With
# Fern Michaels

# More Zebra Regency Romances